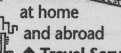

Enrollment Form

☐ **Yes!** I WANT TO BE A *Privileged Woman.*

Enclosed is one *PAGES & PRIVILEGES*™ Proof of Purchase from any Harlequin or Silhouette book currently for sale in stores (Proofs of Purchase are found on the back pages of books) and the store cash register receipt. Please enroll me in *PAGES & PRIVILEGES*™. Send my Welcome Kit and FREE Gifts – and activate my FREE benefits – immediately.

More great gifts and benefits to come.

NAME (please print)

ADDRESS   APT. NO

CITY   STATE   ZIP/POSTAL CODE

PROOF OF PURCHASE ONLY	**NO CLUB!** **NO COMMITMENT!** Just one purchase brings you great Free Gifts and Benefits!

Please allow 6-8 weeks for delivery. Quantities are limited. We reserve the right to substitute items. Enroll before October 31, 1995 and receive one full year of benefits.

Name of store where this book was purchased_____

Date of purchase_____

Type of store:

☐ Bookstore   ☐ Supermarket   ☐ Drugstore

☐ Dept. or discount store (e.g. K-Mart or Walmart)

☐ Other (specify)_____

Which Harlequin or Silhouette series do you usually read?

_____

Complete and mail with one Proof of Purchase and store receipt to:

U.S.: *PAGES & PRIVILEGES*™, P.O. Box 1960, Danbury, CT 06813-1960

Canada: *PAGES & PRIVILEGES*™, 49-6A The Donway West, P.O. 813, North York, ON M3C 2E8

HP-PP6B

"You know not what you ask."

"So you decide for me," she mocked. "Where is the sharing of minds and hearts in that?"

"There are matters of far greater consequence than you," he snapped.

She ignored that and advanced on him, adrenaline running high, determined on *touching* him again. "All the time in the world will not win my trust if you won't give me yours. Or is your plan simply to dominate me, and keep yourself apart?"

For the first time she saw conflict in his eyes, a dark raging turbulence that coalesced into one searing need. "I am tired of being without a true companion."

"So am I," she whispered, her heart turning over at the vulnerability he revealed.

EMMA DARCY nearly became an actress, until her fiancé declared he preferred to attend the theater with her. She became a wife and mother. Later, she took up oil painting—unsuccessfully, she remarks. Then she tried architecture, designing the family home in New South Wales, Australia. Next came romance writing—"the hardest and most challenging of all the activities," she confesses.

Books by Emma Darcy

HARLEQUIN PRESENTS
1536—AN IMPOSSIBLE DREAM
1632—THE SHINING OF LOVE
1659—A WEDDING TO REMEMBER
1679—IN NEED OF A WIFE
1721—BURNING WITH PASSION
1745—THE FATHERHOOD AFFAIR

EMMA DARCY

Climax of Passion

Harlequin Books

TORONTO • NEW YORK • LONDON
AMSTERDAM • PARIS • SYDNEY • HAMBURG
STOCKHOLM • ATHENS • TOKYO • MILAN
MADRID • WARSAW • BUDAPEST • AUCKLAND

To Linda McQueen,
for her love of words and getting it right

ISBN 0-373-11771-X

CLIMAX OF PASSION

First North American Publication 1995.

Copyright © 1995 by Emma Darcy.

CHAPTER ONE

XA SHIRAQ was notable for many things.

The impression that most people took away with them was of a penetrating gaze that seemed to strip souls bare.

His eyes were stygian black and deeply socketed. It was said they could see through any duplicity. They could burn with the heat of the desert or be as cold and cutting as the wind from the topmost peaks of the Atlas Mountains in the freezing heart of winter. They revealed nothing, yet they knew everything.

He had not inherited the Sheikhdom of Xabia. He had won the right to rule through the sheer force of his will and character. He retained and increased his power by not letting anything escape his notice. His vigilance over matters that others might regard as of little consequence, was legendary. Its effect was that Xa Shiraq was never surprised. He had no intention of ever being surprised.

'Tell me about the geologist's daughter,' he commanded of Kozim, his closest aide.

'No...o...o, ah...problem,' came the habitual singsong reply.

A slicing flash of black eyes was enough for Kozim to clear his throat and bring forth a flurry of detail.

'She is still at the hotel in Fisa, working front of house. She is in charge of reservations. There is a complaint lodged against her. She will not last.'

Xa Shiraq's long, supple fingers tapped a thoughtful rhythm on the armrest of his chair. 'Why did she take the position? Why has she stayed? With her qualifications she could have done better. It makes no sense unless my suspicion has substance. Each step...one step closer.'

'She has applied for a transfer to Bejos,' Kozim added as a possible point of interest.

'Ah!' It was the sound of satisfaction. 'So the purpose reveals itself beyond all reasonable doubt. She is a woman of remarkable determination.' He looked sharply at Kozim. 'If application is made for entry to Xabia, it is to be refused.'

'I will see to it immediately,' Kozim said with fervour, hiding his surprise at such a leap in anticipation.

'Never believe in coincidence, Kozim. Has the transfer to Bejos been granted?'

'No, Your Excellency. It was blocked by the assistant manager at Fisa.'

'For what reason?'

'He claims unsuitability on the grounds that she is a striking blonde and may draw troublesome attention at the Bejos hotel.' Kozim shrugged. 'That is what he says officially.'

'And unofficially?' the sheikh prompted.

'It is inferred that there are more personal reasons.'

The sheikh sat back, hooding his eyes. 'Correct me if I'm wrong, but isn't the Fisa hotel one of the poorest performers in the Oasis chain?'

'You are not wrong, Your Excellency,' Kozim quickly assured him. 'It has one of the lowest occupancy rates.'

'There have been a number of complaints about the hotel,' the sheikh said broodingly.

Kozim didn't know of any. His ignorance did not disturb him. It was not unusual for him not to know what the sheikh knew. Xa Shiraq had many sources of information.

The fingers tapped again. 'I will act. I can kill two birds with one arrow.'

Kozim had no idea what the sheikh meant, but he was glad he was not going to be on the receiving end of the arrow that would undoubtedly reach its targets with deadly accuracy. He was glad he had no connection whatsoever to the running of the Oasis Hotel at Fisa. He was glad he was not the geologist's daughter.

CHAPTER TWO

AMANDA Buchanan thought she had developed a thick enough skin to withstand most of the put-down jokes that came her way. Normally, she let them flow past her like water off a duck's back. After all, she had been born with three strikes against her. Her mother had been Polish, her father Irish, and she was a natural blonde.

The latest rash of 'dumb blonde' jokes was the most belittling she had so far encountered. It was almost enough to drive her into dying her hair black. Her stubborn sense of self-worth, however, would not countenance any backing off from who and what she was. Apart from which, it would give her snide detractors the satisfaction of knowing they had got to her.

One day, she vowed, she would make a lot of people eat their words. Not only on her own account, but on her father's. Amanda wasn't quite sure how she was going to achieve that end, but working for the Oasis chain of hotels had seemed a likely step in the right direction. What she needed to do was get into a high level management position which might...just might...open the door to where she wanted to go.

In the meantime, she had to grit her teeth and suffer the assistant manager's malicious manner and

8

spite in putting her down in every possible way he could conceive.

She knew why he did it. It was a payback for her lack of interest in him as a man. Charles Arnold combined a huge ego with small performance. His principal aim in life was to downgrade everybody to his own level so that he could feel superior. He had no idea how badly it reflected on himself and on his job.

If Amanda had been willing to accommodate him, his attitude and that of the male staff would have been very different. A shudder of revulsion ran through her at the mere thought of submitting to Charles Arnold's touch. That was never going to happen, no matter what subtle or unsubtle pressure he brought to bear. As it was, the other staff took their lead from him, having their bit of 'fun' with her, knowing they were completely safe from any complaint of harassment.

There was only one person who could have fixed the situation for Amanda, and that was the vague, shadowy figure of Xa Shiraq, the owner of the Oasis chain. It was said that he held all the key decisions regarding personnel in his own hands. He was never around. He was never seen. There were doubts he really existed.

Amanda knew better. When her father lay dying in her arms, revealing what had happened in halting, stumbling words...it left no doubt in Amanda's mind that Xa Shiraq existed.

This was the third Oasis Hotel Amanda had worked in. The mysterious owner had not once made an appearance at any of them. Promotions and sackings were done by impersonal faxes, never in person. Despite this lack of any substantial evidence of his actual presence, her father's assurance and certainty had convinced Amanda that Xa Shiraq was indeed flesh and blood reality.

Her belief, however, was of no help to her in her present situation. It was difficult to keep her cool while she burned with the injustice of what was happening to her, but Amanda was determined not to put a foot wrong.

Soon, very soon, she hoped, her transfer to the Oasis Hotel in Bejos would come through. Then she would be one step closer to her real goal, one more step removed from her persecutors. Charles Arnold and his minions would then become so much flotsam that she could jettison from her life.

A telephone call claimed her attention. She lifted the receiver and projected a pleasant, welcoming note into her voice. 'Good morning. The Oasis Hotel. Reservations.'

'Is the Presidential Suite available tonight?' a male voice inquired without preamble.

'Just a moment, sir, I'll check it on the computer.'

Amanda knew perfectly well that the most expensive suite in the hotel was vacant. In the five months she had worked here, it had been occupied only seven times. On every one of these occasions it had been given to bridal couples on a one-night complimentary basis as an inducement for the booking of the wedding reception. No-one had paid good money for it. This was not something the hotel management wanted broadcast to the rest of the world.

'Yes, sir, it is available,' she said after a suitable pause. 'For how long would you like to make a reservation?'

'For how long will it be available?'

Amanda chose an encouraging reply. 'We would do our very best to ensure you have undisturbed occupancy for as long as you require.'

There was no response. The click of a receiver being quietly replaced sent a highly disquieting tingle down Amanda's spine. Had someone been testing her, checking that she was not too free with information about bookings? There had been one fabricated complaint lodged against her, engineered by Charles Arnold to demonstrate the cost of his displeasure.

She assured herself there had been nothing to criticise in her handling of the call. If anyone had been playing funny games she'd given them no rope to hang her with. Nevertheless, the incident nagged at her mind long after she should have dismissed it.

It was the voice that had made her think the caller was genuine in his inquiry about the Presidential Suite. A hard, distinctive voice with a ring of arrogance about it. The kind of voice one instinctively associated with a position of power or wealth. A voice that expected requests to be automatically carried out to the letter, yet lacking any trace of the spoilt petulance that came from people born to riches.

It had been rude of him, though, to leave her hanging like that on the telephone. The courtesy of a 'Thank you' would have cost him nothing. Amanda decided if she ever met the man behind that voice, she would know him immediately. She knew how she would treat him, too.

While giving him all the courtesy and attention demanded by her job, she would maintain considerable reserve, aplomb, dignity and aloofness. A rueful smile flitted over her lips. More likely than not, he wouldn't notice her manner. He was probably the type of person who didn't acknowledge anyone who was not his peer.

A busload of tourists trailed in en masse for a three-night stopover. Charles Arnold put in an officious appearance, extolling the facilities of the hotel to the tour leader. Amanda helped with the process of checking everyone in and dispensing room keys.

She saw the man come in.

He emerged from the huge revolving door that gave entrance to the foyer and paused, taking in the melee around the front desk. There was something about him that arrested Amanda's attention. Not his clothes. They were unremarkable; a white open-necked shirt, beige linen jacket, brown trousers. Not his looks. She had seen more handsome men. He was tall and lean, like an athlete honed to perfection. Amanda had seen that before with the Olympic Games team.

It was his stillness, his ability to concentrate and focus his full attention that was unusual. He observed the crowd of tourists and the piles of luggage strewn around the foyer in careless disarray. Amanda knew immediately that if he had been tour leader there would have been no carelessness and no disarray.

The signs of contempt in his eyes and on his face were marginal, but they were there. He was a man born to organise—people, places, things. He absorbed everything down to the minutest detail.

Amanda found his intensity disquieting. Making judgements, she thought, and not favorable ones.

'Have any messages come in for me? My name is...'

Amanda smiled at the woman who had addressed her and obligingly checked for messages. When she darted another glance at the man, she found he had moved to the lounge setting beside the fountain. He was seated in an armchair that faced the reception desk. He had not picked up a newspaper or magazine to idle away the time. He was watching Charles Arnold's effusive performance with the tour leader in the same way as a hawk watched a sparrow.

Again Amanda was struck by his stillness. Very few people could control and maintain immobility for more than a few seconds. It took the kind of discipline and training of both mind and body that Amanda associated with the ceremonial guards outside Windsor Castle in England. Yet she felt intuitively that this was not a man who took orders. He gave them. He was waiting...waiting for the right moment to take command.

It was difficult to guess his age. He had taut, smooth, dark olive skin stretched over strongly delineated bones; skin unmarked, unblemished, like polished wood—an ageless face.

There was no grey in his black hair. It was thick and straight and shiny, as shiny as his deeply set black eyes. He had certainly reached the age of maturity but whether he was as young as thirty or a decade or more older, Amanda found it impossible to decide.

Handsome was not the right word for him. He was distinctive. Her mind kept coming back to *commanding* as she dealt with other requests and inquiries from the party of tourists. He was also disturbing. Very disturbing. So disturbing that Amanda had a serious difficulty in tearing her eyes away from him.

Briefly he caught her glance, held it, and dismissed it.

Amanda's heart skipped a beat. By the intense application of willpower she managed to wrest her attention back to what she was supposed to be doing. What had happened was more than disturbing. She had never reacted like this before in her life.

The worst part of the situation was that Amanda was convinced that this man, this outsider, this stranger had read every thought that had flashed through her mind. He knew, and understood, and did not care. He had come across similar situations many times in his life.

She was nothing new to him. No-one to hold his interest. Amanda was used to put-downs. It was silly to let it hurt, yet for some unfathomable reason, coming from him, it did.

His attention had switched back to Charles Arnold. His stillness was minimally broken. The fingers of his right hand began to tap across the end of the armrest in a steadily paced rhythm as though he was counting.

The tour leader called for attention and gave schedule details, stipulating the time for the next group meeting in the foyer. The crowd dispersed, picking up luggage, heading for the elevators and the rooms allotted to them.

Amanda automatically tensed as Charles Arnold chose to join her behind the front desk, a look of smug satisfaction centered on his face. 'Well, that should put the numbers up. What's the intake for today, Mandy?'

Amanda gritted her teeth and pressed the keys to bring up the total on the computer. She hated the way he drawled his version of her name, making her sound like some brainless kewpie doll. She also hated the way he crowded her as he looked over her shoulder at the monitor screen, not exactly touching, but only a breath away. A hot breath. A breath that made her skin crawl.

'Not bad,' he commented. 'I've done well. A pity everyone else can't do as well. Now do a breakdown on singles, doubles and suites.'

Her fingers faltered and stopped as she had the strangest feeling of being gripped by some alien force. She looked up. The man from the armchair was walking towards the desk, his black eyes focused directly on her, giving her more concentrated attention, seeming to absorb all that she was.

Amanda's heart skittered into a faster beat. He hadn't dismissed her, after all. She could not help wondering what he saw, how she was adding up in his mind, how he would attempt to organise her.

He probably thought her a soft pale creature compared to himself. Although her fair complexion had acquired a light golden tan in the tropical sunshine at Fisa, this only tended to accentuate the bright clarity of her aquamarine eyes, and made her long ash-blonde hair look whiter than it was, especially against the black suit that was the standard hotel uniform for her position.

Amanda was no fragile flower, but her facial features did have a delicate femininity, and she was slender and softly curved. Her physical appearance gave many men, men like Charles Arnold, the impression that she would be malleable and easy to manage. Amanda was quite happy for them to think so. Until such time as they crossed her mental line of what she considered wrong for her, anyone could think what they liked.

'I have not been attended to.'

The sharp, demanding edge to the stranger's voice made the statement sound like the most culpable crime against responsibility since the captain of the *Titanic* ordered full steam ahead.

Amanda's fanciful speculations came to a dead halt. Her mind did an abrupt about-turn. She knew that voice. She had already heard it once today. *This man owed her an apology for his rudeness on the telephone.*

Charles Arnold gave the gentleman a perfunctory glance. 'Everyone has to take their turn here, sir,' he said brightly. 'We'll be with you in just a moment.'

In typically arrogant dismissal of anyone who impinged on his personal priorities, Charles turned back to Amanda. 'Well, get on with it. The figures, please, Mandy,' he urged. Then in an insultingly condescending tone, he instructed, 'Put your finger on the Enter key and...'

'No! You will not touch the Enter key.'

The tone of absolute authority shivered through the air-conditioned atmosphere. Amanda had been right about one thing. The owner of the voice did not like having his orders disobeyed. He probably had an intense dislike for the word 'no', as well. Unless it was he who was using it.

She did her best to retrieve the situation. 'We have a new arrival, Mr Arnold,' she stated quietly. 'Perhaps we could attend to him first.'

She flashed the stranger a quick glance, all ideas of aloofness, reserve, dignity and aplomb forgotten for the moment. She could not afford to have another complaint lodged against her. Her look carried a simple message. It said, please be aware that you are placing me in a difficult situation.

The man's eyelids lowered fractionally for the briefest of moments, as if he had received her message, understood it completely, but nothing would divert him from the course of action he had chosen.

'Don't give me your dizzy blonde act, Mandy,' Charles Arnold said, having missed the byplay between Amanda and the newly arrived guest. 'These figures are important to me. My next promotion depends on them.'

'I will have the Presidential Suite.'

That arrested Charles Arnold's attention. Amanda hadn't told him about the earlier inquiry. A paying customer in the Presidential Suite was a feather in any management cap. The dangling prize effected a complete reversal of attitude in Charles Arnold.

'You are very welcome, sir.'

Pure smarmy syrup, Amanda thought, barely hiding her disgust as the sucking up act began.

'We will attend to your every need immediately. Most regrettable that you've been kept waiting. If you'd alerted us earlier . . . However, we shall make generous amends. A porter for your luggage, sir? Any special refreshment you'd like in your suite? I'll have your butler rung so it can be delivered while we...uh...take reservation details. Your name, sir?'

'It is not necessary for you to know my name.' It was a cold rebuff. The stranger, who was apparently intent on remaining a stranger, withdrew a folded sheet of paper from the inner pocket of his sports jacket and tossed it onto the desk. 'This is all you need to know.'

Amanda watched Charles Arnold unfold the paper. It was thick, creamy, expensive. Her breath caught in her throat as she saw the emblem at the top of the page. She was not in a position to read the typed lines underneath, but that notepaper, that emblem, represented the man she most wanted to reach.

She had seen it before amongst her father's papers...the personal insignia of the Sheikh of Xabia...a gyrfalcon at full wing, its talons poised ready to strike.

Her stomach seemed to turn over. Despite a sudden and debilitating feeling of weakness in her bones, Amanda forced herself to look once more at the commanding, ageless face in front of her. Was he...could he possibly be...Xa Shiraq himself?

CHAPTER THREE

No SOONER had the electric thought gripped Amanda's mind, than a wash of common sense defused it. No way would Xa Shiraq arrive at any hotel as casually as this man had, or dressed as this man was. The Sheikh of Xabia would have a retinue, bodyguard. He wouldn't wait for anything. He'd be waited on hand and foot!

'This isn't signed,' Charles Arnold said huffily. 'Anyone could have typed those words. I do not consider it an authorisation to give you complimentary use of our Presidential Suite. Unless you can produce more than that, sir...' he tossed the page back onto the desk in contemptuous rejection '...you are wasting our time.'

It gave Amanda the opportunity to read what was written on the page. The message was short and succinct.

> By order of Xa Shiraq, the bearer of this note is entitled to have any request within my jurisdiction fulfilled.

Her mind dizzied again with the enormity of what was happening in front of her. This man was certainly not Xa Shiraq but he had to be important to have such a note. He could be one of Xa Shiraq's three great supporters, all military men who by their

20

loyalty and skill had helped Xa Shiraq win the sheikhdom in the first place. There was Jebel Haffa and...

Amanda took a deep breath. She pulled her mind into order. This man could lead her to one of her primary goals, the secretive and elusive Xa Shiraq himself.

'You question its authenticity?' The icy sting in his voice was not propitious to any pact of friendship.

'Naturally a man in my position of authority has to do so,' Charles Arnold observed coldly.

On the surface, it was a reasonable statement. It was true, Amanda reflected, that anyone with access to that particular notepaper could have written the letter. The hotel had discreet procedures for checking authenticity and credit ratings for guests. These procedures should now be followed.

'Perhaps...' she began.

Charles Arnold cut her short. 'The figures please, Mandy.'

He turned back to the stranger, intent on cutting this arrogant foreigner down to his own level. Amanda had seen it all before. 'As I've already said, anyone could have typed this order...'

'Who would dare?'

The challenge sent a quiver through Amanda. Her gaze flew up to the hard commanding face. This man had to be close to Xa Shiraq. Very close. And his eyes missed nothing. How could she possibly get close to him? Yet if she could...

must... her pulse quickened. Given half an opportunity... and she would leap at it.

'I will not fall prey to a cheap confidence trick,' Charles Arnold scoffed, losing control of the situation but reasserting his sense of superiority.

To reinforce it even further, he picked up the typewritten authorisation, held it gingerly by one corner as though it were contaminated, slowly drifted it to a position above the disposal bin, then released his grip. The letter floated down to join the rest of the garbage paper in the bin.

'That,' said Charles Arnold with satisfaction, 'is what I think of that.' As far as he was concerned, he had just won his encounter with the stranger.

The stranger said nothing. The black blaze of his eyes would have incinerated most people but his target was cocooned in self-importance. He lifted a hand. Amanda prayed for more time. The hand moved up to shoulder height as though he intended to slap it onto the counter. But it did not descend.

A man loitering near the fountain moved abruptly into a brisk walk towards the desk. He wore a black suit and carried a black leather attaché case. Amanda recognised him as a guest who had booked in two days ago, a Mr Kozim from Bejos, a rather portly, middle-aged man, darker in skin tone than the stranger in front of her and more obviously of Middle Eastern origins.

He came to a halt beside the stranger who then lowered his hand but did not so much as glance at the man who had responded to his signal. Mr Kozim placed his attaché case on the desk, opened it, removed a typed page with the letterhead of the Oasis chain, and passed it to Charles Arnold.

'For legal purposes you will find that document is signed by Jebel Haffa,' the stranger stated bitingly. 'I hope you will recognise his signature.'

Charles Arnold began sputtering. 'What is the meaning of this? It can't be . . .'

'It means that as of this moment you are relieved of your duties as assistant manager of this hotel,' came the hard, relentless reply. 'You are no longer employed here. You have no further involvement with the Oasis chain.'

'We'll see about that,' Charles Arnold blustered. 'I'm calling the general manager.'

'That would be expedient.'

Amanda reached for the phone. Charles Arnold beat her to it. This call was too important to be entrusted to a menial like Amanda.

Charles Arnold protested his fate in acrimonious terms.

Amanda's mind whirled.

Charles Arnold had given her hell. He had fabricated a complaint against her. He had harassed and hounded her, belittled and demeaned her, persecuted her to the limits of endurance.

The stranger had told her not to do it.

She ignored the order.

Amanda's need to even the score between herself and Charles Arnold was a stronger force.

She pressed the Enter key.

She turned to face Charles Arnold directly, her gaze level, her voice level, her manner civil and courteous, her bearing reserved, dignified and aloof.

'You wanted these figures, sir,' she said evenly. 'For your promotion, sir.'

'You dumb stupid blonde bitch!' Charles Arnold snorted like a chained killer dog deprived of its prey.

'I'm sorry I'm a dumb stupid blonde bitch, sir,' she said, taking intense pride in appearing totally unruffled. There was no way Charles Arnold could ever hurt her again. She had given him the *coup de grâce*. There would be no festering wounds left over from this encounter. She would not spend any more nights blistering over her resentments at his petty tyranny.

She turned slowly towards the stranger and caught the look in his eyes. It took her breath away. She had seen desire before in men's eyes. Occasionally she had seen lust. She had never before confronted a message of such blazing conviction. *I want you*, his eyes said. *I'll have you. And what I have I keep.*

She saw it, felt it, yet it was over in an instant. A shutter snapped closed. The blaze was gone, replaced by impenetrable darkness.

The muscles of her stomach clenched. Her thighs tightened in response. Her eyelids dropped fractionally as his own had done previously, but her facade of cool composure did not falter.

The stranger and Mr Kozim ignored every word uttered by Charles Arnold. Like water off a duck's back, Amanda thought. Xa Shiraq's hatchet man and his secretary had probably arranged this scene long before it was enacted.

She felt no sympathy for Charles Arnold. After his persecution of her, he deserved none. She was relieved at his removal from the staff.

The general manager made his entrance, coming in behind the front desk to line up beside his chief assistant and lend authoritative support. 'What is the problem?' he demanded in frowning inquiry.

'Did you employ this man?' Mr Kozim asked, pointing at Charles Arnold.

'I most certainly did,' the manager replied happily.

'Here is an official letter, relieving you of your position and responsibilities within the Oasis chain,' Mr Kozim said affably. He reached inside his briefcase, scanned the contents of a letter, and passed it to the general manager. 'You will note it is signed by Jebel Haffa,' Mr Kozim added idly.

'You...you can't do this...' The words stuttered out.

'It's done,' the voice of the stranger cut in peremptorily.

'But you have no senior management left...you'll need us.'

'It has been taken care of. Miss Buchanan...' His gaze swung to her.

Amanda was astonished. 'You know my name.'

'I know *everything*,' he said with becoming modesty, 'that is important to me.'

Amanda pulled herself together. 'Yes, sir,' she said with becoming deference. 'I'm sure you do.'

'Miss Buchanan, there is a letter for you.' The stranger nodded to Mr Kozim whose hand dived into the attaché case.

Amanda's heart sank. The fabricated complaint had served its purpose. Her future plans were shattered, her goals more unattainable than ever.

She noted the triumphant smirk on Charles Arnold's face. Despite his immense chagrin at his own predicament, nothing diluted his pleasure in bringing someone else down.

She forced herself to take the letter. Her hands felt nerveless, divorced from her body. The words printed on the page were scrambled and incomprehensible. She concentrated her attention, and deciphered what was written.

By the order of Xa Shiraq, Miss Amanda Buchanan is appointed general manager of the Oasis Hotel at Fisa, commencing at 3 o'clock on...

The date followed, and beneath the date was the signature of Jebel Haffa.

Her hand trembled at the import of that briefly stated command. Her eyes flew to the wall clock. It was exactly three o'clock. Clockwork precision. A little masterpiece of organisation and planning, everything accounted for.

'Your new assistants will arrive within the hour.'

Her gaze swung back to the man who served Xa Shiraq with such unswerving commitment to his orders. He did not ask her whether she would take the job. He knew she would.

'Kozim, you will accompany these two gentlemen to their respective offices in order to clear their desks,' was his next command.

Amanda watched them go, their numb disbelief equalled only by her own.

'You have two minutes to effect a temporary re-organisation.' This command was directed at her, galvanising her attention. The black eyes glinted with unyielding purpose. 'Then you will escort me to the Presidential Suite.'

'Very well, sir,' Amanda said with all the aplomb she could muster. She had to think quickly. The front desk had to be restaffed. The rest could wait.

She dialled the office secretary. 'Please come and fill in at the front desk,' she commanded. The man in front of her, listening to what was going on, was ruthless.

She met resistance. 'That's not in my job description.'

'If you're not here in one minute you won't have a job.'

'Mr Arnold said...'

'Mr Arnold has been relieved of all duties.'

Amanda put the receiver down. Next was house-keeping. She organised butler service for the Presidential Suite. She commandeered an affable young waiter for the front desk in case the secretary didn't turn up.

There was something else she had to do. She had to find out the name of the man in front of her, and what his connection was to Xa Shiraq.

Amanda headed for the computer. 'What name will I use for your reservation, sir?' she asked sweetly.

'Complimentary Upgrade,' he replied laconically.

Amanda could play word games too. Some boldness was called for if she was to get what she wanted. 'Very good, sir. That's no trouble, sir. First name is Complimentary, surname is Upgrade.' She typed the letters out on the keyboard, glanced up at him to see how he took that.

A quirk at the corner of his mouth told her he found it rather droll.

'Your reservation is complete, sir. I'm now ready to escort you to the Presidential Suite.'

He looked at his wristwatch. 'That's very good, Miss Buchanan. You had ten seconds to spare.'

'In that case, sir, I'll use the time to assemble the paperwork relating to this afternoon's activities.'

Amanda hurriedly assembled all the letters lying around. The men had not bothered to take their dismissal notices with them. She deposited them in the bottom of the cashier's register. They would be safe there until she could find time to get back to them.

'Time's up.'

There was no demand in his voice, nothing peremptory. Amanda knew as well as he did she had satisfied every demand he had placed upon her. So far. How long that would last...

'Do you have any luggage?'

'None that is of concern to the hotel.'

'Thank you, Mr Upgrade,' she challenged him. 'It's my pleasure to escort you to your suite.'

He looked at her in reassessment, decided to let the challenge go unremarked.

'I hope it will be a pleasure, Miss Buchanan,' he said mildly. 'A great pleasure.'

Amanda looked at him again. A prickle of danger ran down her spine. She was quite certain that the pleasure Upgrade had in his mind was not identical to the pleasure she had in hers. She needed to get close to this man, but not *that* close!

CHAPTER FOUR

HE HAD stipulated nine o'clock.

Amanda paced her room, waiting for the last few minutes to tick by before she had to face the man in the Presidential Suite again. She felt too on edge to sit down. Impossible to relax. So much depended upon what happened in the next hour.

He was a reasonable man, she assured herself. He hadn't tried to detain her this afternoon. He had not said anything suggestive, nor made any move that could be interpreted as taking a liberty. He had agreed she had many pressing duties as the new general manager...and in the same breath, made this appointment for a discussion on her future.

Nine o'clock was not an unreasonable time. It had given her six hours to deal with whatever problems arose from the shock departure of the senior management and her startling promotion to the top rank. Implicit in that choice of hour, however, was the understanding that Amanda's time was his, free of all interruptions. Amanda could not fool herself that he only wanted to talk business with her.

She couldn't forget that brief blaze of searing desire this afternoon. She couldn't deny the fascination he exerted on her. She was going to be in deep trouble if he rejected the schedule she had set in place.

Surely, as a reasonable man, he would accept what she had arranged. All the preparations had been made. She had covered every contingency. He couldn't take offence at what she had done for him and it gave her a smooth getaway.

The only problem was...she had never met anyone like this man before. He affected her in ways...but there was no future in dwelling on that. If she gave in to this...attraction...compulsion... she would end up in his power, and where would that lead?

Amanda shook her head. It was too dangerous. However tempting it was to have the experience, to know all that *he* was, she had no doubt it would mean ceding control to him. And that she would not do.

Her decisions were made. She could not afford to waver from her chosen course. She had to seize the authority she now had and use it while time was still on her side. It was daring, so daring her heart had been pumping overtime ever since she had thought of it. Once she started there could be no stopping, no turning back. Her actions would be irreversible.

But first she had to face *him*.

She checked her watch. It was time to move. Punctuality was mandatory. She left her room and headed for the elevators. Her legs felt shaky. She steeled her mind to cope with the situation. She only had to get through one hour with him. She could keep her wits about her for one short hour.

She took deep, calming breaths as she rode up to the top floor. Her legs were much steadier on her walk to the door of the Presidential Suite. It was precisely nine o'clock as she pressed the buzzer to announce her arrival.

The door clicked open. 'Good evening,' she said to the butler.

'I'm just leaving, Miss Buchanan. I've served the champagne.'

'Thank you,' she said on a note of resignation. The butler had obviously been given his orders. Mr Complimentary Upgrade meant to have her to himself, no third party around to inhibit whatever he wanted to happen between them.

The butler stood aside to let her through, and then, empty tray in hand, made his departure.

Amanda was immediately aware that the rooms beyond the vestibule were dimly lit. Champagne...soft lights...but the Presidential Suite was very large. Like a penthouse really. She had plenty of space to move around in.

Besides, this man was not the type to rush anything. Not something he wanted. He would wait patiently, wanting it all precisely as he planned it. Step by step. Relentless and ruthless in his execution.

Amanda shivered, then took firm control of herself. Nothing was going to happen that she didn't want to happen. Determined to hold her own against this disturbing man, she set forth into the living room, back straight, chin up, a brave smile of confidence hovering on her lips. She felt rather foolish when he wasn't there to greet her.

The table lamps on either side of the white leather lounge setting were switched on. Spotlit by one was a silver ice bucket containing a bottle of champagne. The cork had been removed and the sparkling fluid poured into two crystal flute glasses.

Amanda's hands clenched. If he was about to appear in something *more comfortable...*

'The stars are brightly shining tonight.'

Amanda almost jumped. His voice was enough of a magnet to draw her gaze instantly to where he stood at the far end of the room, a darker shadow amongst the shadows beyond the long expanse of glass that faced the balcony.

It made Amanda acutely conscious of being in a pool of light, of having been observed without her knowledge. He would have noted she was still in her black suit, noted the body language that revealed her inner tension, and had probably already decided how best to deal with the situation. She felt at a distinct disadvantage.

'It's a good omen,' he said softly. 'I like watching the stars.'

'Do you? I find a great deal of pleasure...' Amanda began, rushing into speech to cover her disquiet, then wishing she'd held her tongue. Pleasure was a word she did not wish to use tonight. 'There is a grandeur and sweep to it,' she acknowledged, trying to put the conversation on an impersonal level.

He left the shadows and strolled towards her, projecting a totally relaxed manner. Amanda was relieved to see he was fully dressed although he had changed his clothes. He wore black. Easier to merge with the night, Amanda thought. Then she saw the sheen of silk in his shirt and knew that his choice had more to do with sensuality than darkness. It was an invitation to touch, to feel, to lose herself in a night with him.

He paused at the table where the drinks were laid out. 'I have taken the liberty of ordering some Dom Perignon to celebrate your promotion,' he said with a smile that was both whimsical and seductive. 'Will you partake of a glass with me?'

He was already having an intoxicating effect on her... a man of mystery, of immense fascination. She couldn't risk heightening it by any relaxation of her defences. 'I don't drink when I'm on duty,' she said quickly.

'And I don't drink at all,' he said slowly. 'Nevertheless, these are challenging times in which we live, Miss Buchanan.'

He picked up the two glasses and brought them to her, standing close, making her extremely conscious of her vulnerable femininity. Something primitive pulsed from this man. It was muted by the civilised clothes, the civilised manner, yet her every instinct recognised the barbarian in him, the hunter, the conqueror, the possessor.

Amanda had the sense, the feeling of potent danger. He was so vibrant, so intensely alive, as though he thrived on challenge, as though it was meat and drink to him, the very essence of life.

'Let us dare to break our own rules,' he tempted softly, his eyes engaging hers with mesmerising directness.

She had to speak, to keep him talking. Only words could battle the effect he was having on her and keep him at a distance. 'Wouldn't that be flirting with chaos? You struck me as a man who appreciates and demands order, Mr Upgrade.'

'Chaos can be brought into order, if the will is strong enough.'

'Do as you will, but I shall not put my sense of order at risk. I prefer to keep my promotion than lose it on a glass of champagne.'

One black eyebrow arched quizzically. 'Surely you make something out of nothing.'

'I find it somewhat surprising that I was chosen for the position of general manager. That was something out of nothing.'

'Call it impulse.'

'With an already signed letter from Jebel Haffa?'

'Xa Shiraq provides for all contingencies.'

'Was it your…impulse…or that of Xa Shiraq?'

He smiled as if at some secret irony. 'All was provided for. You need to know nothing more.'

'What does Xa Shiraq know of me?' she asked boldly.

'Everything and nothing.'

'Can you stop speaking in paradoxes and talk directly?'

He laughed softly, completely in control of the situation. 'Yes and no,' he replied.

Amanda realised he was toying with her, deliberately provoking her, inciting her to some rash step. She was equally determined not to be provoked, not to be played or toyed with, not to take some hasty, rash step.

'An admirable response,' she retorted dryly, 'which answers all my questions.'

He hadn't expected that. He eyed her again, let his gaze slide down her body, then turned aside to set the glasses back on the table, having abandoned any further thought of pressing the champagne on her and apparently not inclined to drink by himself. 'I believe what I see and feel. I believe in myself, Miss Buchanan,' he said quietly.

The light from the table lamp played over his chin and cheekbones and she thought he had the kind of profile that had once been struck on ancient coins, a noble, immortal face. Then he straightened up and the illusion was lost in the vital furnace of his eyes, desire that curled around her, encompassed her, and tugged on something basic inside her that made Amanda feel alarmingly out of control.

'As deeply and with as much conviction as you believe in yourself, and in what you see and feel,' he said, his voice a low velvet throb.

How did he know that? Could he see into her mind and heart?

'You judge character quickly, Mr Upgrade,' she remarked, knowing she must keep him talking, keep him at a safe distance.

His hands were free now, free to touch . . . and if he touched . . . She felt her skin yearning for it, her palms itching for it. Never before had her body reacted like this to a man, and she didn't even know who he was. Didn't want to know. If he gave her his name, his identity, she suspected that would make him a more powerful memory. Unforgettable.

'One look at a person and much is revealed. You were described to me as a striking blonde. That suggests certain images. None of them was accurate.'

'How do you judge me?' she asked, too intrigued not to satisfy her curiosity.

'To you, purpose outweighs feminine vanity. You have no desire to heighten sexual attraction. You are sensual. Your hair is long, beautifully fair, and uncompromisingly straight. That strengthens your charisma. Frequent visits to a hairdressing salon do not interest you. The fringe is neat and tidy. From that I conclude it is an easy solution to keeping the long fall from intruding on your face. There is no artifice or disguise. Your vision is not obscured. Practical. Efficient. You think of yourself as a person first, a woman second. Your inner needs are more important to you than drawing attention from men. An admirable quality indeed.'

Amanda was stunned by the truths he had so easily perceived. She had gone past the point of wanting to attract men. She had concluded years ago, after a number of disillusioning disappointments, that if a Mr Right did come along, it would happen quite naturally without any need for her to do anything except be herself.

She was not desperate for a man. She had other things to do that were important to her. And she was not about to let *this* man stand in her way, no matter how fascinating she found him. He could not be right for her even though...no, it was impossible.

'Are you a hairdresser by trade, Mr Upgrade?' she mocked at him, trying to restore her equilibrium.

'I have shorn many sheep,' he mocked back, 'but none as fair as you.'

'If you see so much in hair, what do you make of my eyes?'

'When they look upon me and shine as brightly as the stars do tonight, I will tell you. In the meantime, let us concentrate upon the draping of your hair down to the soft, supple swell of your breasts...'

His gaze followed his words and Amanda had the prickling sensation of her nipples pushing against the lace fabric of her bra. The lace felt tight, constrictive, abrasive. She wondered what it would be like having his hands cupping her swelling breasts and was shocked at the vividness of the image that leapt into her mind, the darker tone of his skin against hers, those long lean fingers closing over her soft flesh, caressing her, sensitising her.

She gave herself a mental shake and was grateful that the black suit was not so form-fitting that he could see the effect he was having on her. 'You judge much from my appearance, Mr Upgrade,' she said dismissively, needing the distraction of some other subject, yet failing to bring her mind to focus on anything other than what he was making her feel.

His eyes simmered up to hers. 'Salome used seven veils to seduce a king's mind. I think you would only need one.'

'I'm not a dancer,' she stated firmly. Nor was she going to try.

He ignored her interjection, pressing the image in his mind into hers. 'A veil in shimmering shades of blue and green and silver...translucent. To match your eyes.'

'My eyes aren't silver,' she said pettishly.

'They are like crystal over water, reflecting many facets, tantalising glimpses of what lies behind them.'

Instinctively Amanda lowered her lashes, afraid of revealing too much, not realising how provocative the action was.

'Ah, yes...the strength of mind is greater,' he said with satisfaction, walking towards her again, diminishing the space between them. 'But it is encased in a woman's body. A body I could bend to my will.'

She stiffened as he reached touching distance. Every nerve in her body twanged with tension, whether from anticipation, excitement or fear, she did not know.

He stopped. 'You have nothing to fear from me, Miss Buchanan.'

She wasn't at all sure of that. She could feel his power draining what strength she had. Her impulses were going haywire.

'I give freely, generously—to the right people,' he said persuasively.

By what standard did he judge the *right* people? Her father had not been considered a *right* person by Xa Shiraq, and since this man carried out Xa Shiraq's orders, perhaps he had been the one who ensured her father's unique discovery went discredited in the eyes of the rest of the world.

'Measure yourself against me,' he invited. 'You are smaller, softer, more slender. Women were made to be partnered by men. They need a man to stand by them, protect them, look after them.'

'An old-fashioned idea,' Amanda protested. 'No longer appropriate.'

'A physical reality. Never dismiss the physical strength of a man and the pleasure it can give, Miss Buchanan. However steely your will, it is not proof against it.'

'Why do you feel it is necessary to tell me what I know?' Amanda asked, holding her ground with increasing difficulty.

'Because you are denying what is self-evident. Mind over matter. But I know what you are feeling, Miss Buchanan. Whether you choose to indulge yourself or not.' His black eyes burned into hers.

'I know what you are feeling. I feel it, too. I think we both will always feel it. And remember it.'

'How can you be so sure?' Her voice was a bare husky whisper.

'Because I have never felt it before,' he murmured.

Her eyes warred with his, fighting the link of intimacy he was forging with her. Amanda was certain of one thing. If she succumbed to this man she would never be herself again. He would dominate. She knew he would. He was that kind of person.

He suddenly laughed and turned aside. 'It is a joke, is it not? A man of my age and experience...to be touched...by you...of all women. Yet touched I am...and there will be a resolution to it, Miss Amanda Buchanan. We have met...as perhaps we were always destined to meet.'

Amanda found her breath whooshing out of her lungs as she watched him stroll to the floor-length windows. Her knees were jelly. She wanted to sag onto the nearest lounge. Only a desperate determination to show no weakness kept her upright. Her dazed mind broke out of its enthralment and groped towards a need to understand this man who touched her in ways she had not thought possible.

'How old are you?'

He did not answer immediately. He stared out at the night sky. 'Sometimes I feel as old as the stars...' slowly he turned to look at her again '...but you stir my youth.'

'So you are both young and old.'

'Yes.'

'I am not of your race or culture,' she reminded him.

His words...*you, of all women*...were still ringing in her ears. He knew as well as she did that a liaison between them would give rise to many problems. Yet she could not deny a thrill of pleasure that she had stirred the youth of this man, more particularly as it was against his will.

'Does that matter? Are we not beyond race and culture?'

'There have been other men in my life.'

He shrugged. 'None that you will remember.'

'I'm not a virgin.'

'How unusual!' His lips curled in a humourless smile. 'Nor am I.'

'You're evading the point,' she insisted accusingly, her face flushing at having to be so direct.

'That you could be no more than one light-of-love in my life?'

'Yes.'

He shook his head. 'That is not worth having. It is not what we're about. It's too easy.'

He moved closer. 'Anything worth having exacts a price. I shall pursue you. I shall try to make you submit to my will. You will do everything in your power to make me submit to yours. It becomes an interesting contest, does it not? Who will win, Miss Buchanan?'

For the first time he touched her, his fingers stroking lightly down her cheek, his eyes illuminated with an invigorated lust for life, lust for her, lust for the contest he envisaged.

'Who will win?' he repeated, his voice a low murmur that pulsed through her veins.

Somehow Amanda dredged up the strength to step back from him. 'I have taken the liberty of ordering you a sumptuous supper, Mr Upgrade.' Her voice sounded thin but she plunged on, defiantly ignoring the gauntlet he had thrown at her feet. 'The finest delicacies the hotel has to offer will be brought to you. For your pleasure. Your great pleasure, I hope. And afterwards a dancer to entertain you. The best dancer in Fisa. I believe she does something with veils. If you'll excuse me, I'll go and ensure that your night here is one of entertainment. A night to remember.'

For the merest fraction of time she saw the flash in his eyes. Not admiration. Respect. It was enough. It sent a thrill of elation surging through Amanda. He had not anticipated such a move from her. Please God, he did not anticipate the next one.

'How thoughtful of you!' he said. 'By all means go, Miss Buchanan. There will be another time for us.'

With the thrill of victory thrumming through her, she turned aside. His next words were quietly spoken, but as a counter-stroke, they were chilling.

'The daughter is more impressive than the father.'

She could not stop herself from looking at him again. The black eyes gleamed their victory. He knew who she was, knew far, far, far too much.

'Goodnight, Mr Upgrade,' she said quickly, and spun on her heel away from him, hoping he had not seen or scented her fear.

Her father had died a broken man.

But she would see justice done to him.

The man in the Presidential Suite did not know it yet, but he had opened the door to Xabia for her. He had opened the door to Xa Shiraq. Let him answer for that, Amanda thought fiercely. Then let him see who would win!

CHAPTER FIVE

Xᴀ Sʜɪʀᴀǫ spoke to Kozim.

'If you wish to see a horse gallop, one must loosen the bridle,' he mused as his fingers tapped out a rhythmic beat on the edge of his chair.

'True. Very true,' Kozim agreed.

'I have loosened the bridle.'

'Wise. Very wise,' Kozim assented. He had no idea what Xa Shiraq was talking about, but as this was usually the case, no great harm was ever done by admiring the sheikh's wisdom.

'Two details were overlooked in the operation at the Fisa Oasis Hotel, Kozim,' the sheikh continued.

This was alarming news indeed. Kozim did not know of any operation where any detail was overlooked. Not only that, but his report to Jebel Haffa had affirmed that the operation was entirely successful. What had gone wrong? Was the fault his?

'I have attended to both details,' Xa Shiraq said. His fingers stopped drumming.

'Then there's no...o...o, ah...problem,' Kozim said in relief.

'Kozim, where would you look if you wanted to find a jewel, a jewel almost beyond all price?'

Xa Shiraq was always asking difficult questions. It posed a problem to Kozim. He shrugged.

45

'Perhaps, in the mountains...' he suggested tentatively.

'Don't be a fool, Kozim.' It was an impatient interruption, not a cutting one. The sheikh's black eyes held a glint of amusement as he enlightened Kozim. 'You only find rare jewels of that quality in trash cans, Kozim.'

Kozim struggled to accept that revelation. It had to be true because Xa Shiraq knew everything. Kozim made a mental note that tomorrow he would have all the trash cans in the sheikhdom searched for jewels.

CHAPTER SIX

THE *cachet blanc* that Amanda had so carefully recovered from the trash can in the reception area at the Oasis Hotel, was better than Aladdin's lamp. All she had to do was produce the magical piece of notepaper bearing the gyrfalcon crest of the Sheikh of Xabia, and not only did doors open, the red carpet was laid out for her.

What wonderful words they were!

By order of Xa Shiraq, the bearer of this note is entitled to have any request within my jurisdiction fulfilled.

A visa for Xabia from the embassy at Bejos had been produced in a flash. She was even given a complimentary first class ticket on the first available flight to Alcabab, the capital of Xabia. No customs check for her at the terminal. She was waved through, or rather bowed through, as though she were royalty.

Mocca had claimed her. He was an enterprising youth who scouted the airport terminal for foreign pigeons waiting to be plucked. In the guise of offering his services to provide any service—any service at all—he had offered himself to Amanda.

47

The clear-eyed limpid innocence, the fresh vitality of his olive skin, helped Amanda to come to
a quick decision.

'I need help,' she declared.

'There is no one better than I with help,' he had
replied with deep fervour to press his claim.
Amanda had shown him the sheikh's note of
authority.

His eyes were larger than saucers and brighter
than a Christmas tree when he read it. He treated
Amanda with something akin to reverence. She
figured she had turned out to be the plumpest,
fattest, most succulent pigeon Mocca had ever
plucked.

Amanda thought she needed one truck. Mocca
opted for three four-wheeled drives, nineteen heavy-
duty trucks and a desert cruiser.

Amanda thought she might need a little mining
equipment. Seven of the trucks were now loaded
with enough TNT, plastic explosive and dynamite
to make a sizable hole in any mountain.

'What about the cost?' Amanda had asked
cautiously.

'No...o...o problem,' Mocca assured her.

Mocca had an incredibly extensive family. It
didn't matter what Amanda requested, Mocca had
an uncle or a brother or a cousin who could provide
it for her.

Mocca had brought up the subject of her bodyguard. He eyed her up and down in dispassionate
assessment. 'You will need two, three men,' he declared. 'Maybe four.'

The number turned out to be fifteen, all Mocca's blood relations. When she accosted him on the subject, Mocca had replied with complete confidence that it was no more than what Xa Shiraq wanted. Mocca displayed an uncanny ability to read Xa Shiraq's mind.

Amanda had to put a stop to it. Her secret foray into the Atlas Mountains was taking on the proportions of a Cecil B. deMille Hollywood extravaganza.

'Where is the money coming from?' she demanded of Mocca.

'It's simple,' he explained. 'I invoice everything to the palace.'

The invoices to the palace must have been flying thick and fast, a veritable flood of invoices which surely had to be brought to the sheikh's attention sooner or later.

Amanda's blood ran cold. She hoped it would not be sooner. She had to get evidence of what her father had found before anyone was aware of what was happening. That not only applied to people in the palace. Amanda was acutely aware that her trail to Alcabab could be easily picked up by the man she had left behind in the Presidential Suite at Fisa.

She had caught the last flight to Bejos on the night he had stated his intention to pursue her. That put her at least twelve hours ahead of him since there had not been another flight until the next day. If the entertainment she had organised for him had gone well, he might not have realised she had slipped the coop for twenty-four hours.

Two days had passed since then. By now he would have discovered at Bejos that she had used the authority that was rightfully his. She didn't know if he would confess what had happened to Xa Shiraq or try to find her first, but she suspected the latter. He had said himself he was a man who made his own rules. Amanda did not doubt that. The strength of his personality still haunted her.

As did his challenge to her.

It went far deeper than a contest of wills.

It forced Amanda to examine what it meant to her to be a woman, and what part a man should play in her life. Was she short-changing herself with mind over matter, repressing basic needs that she had found easier not to dwell on? Perhaps she was blocking off something more wonderful than she had ever dreamed of.

When he had touched her…and before that…the way his presence had somehow infiltrated her, tugging on feelings that both excited and frightened her…was she being a coward to deny what might happen with him?

It was not only the heat in Alcabab that kept her awake and restless at night, yet in the end common sense always re-asserted itself. It would be all too easy to slip into a dangerous, exhilarating affair, but the letdown would inevitably come and it would probably take years to get over the emotional scarring. Or was she too frightened, too cautious? Perhaps if the opportunity came again, she should seize it.

As for his pursuit of her, he would have a difficult job finding her in Alcabab, Amanda assured herself. At her request, Mocca had found her an apartment. If Mr Complimentary Upgrade was scouring hotel registers for her name and a person of her description, he would meet with nothing but frustration.

In the meantime, her purchases were so outrageous they could not be overlooked by the palace accountants for long. Xa Shiraq would inevitably demand to know who was using his money and authority to buy such things. Once her identity was known, he would have Patrick Buchanan's daughter brought to him. She would then have the opportunity to demand that he rectify the damage done to her father's reputation. But not before she had the evidence.

Amanda decided she must get out of Alcabab as soon as possible. The longer she stayed in the capital the higher the risk that she would be found by the man pursuing her. He knew whose daughter she was. Her purchases were all aimed at a geology expedition. He was quite capable of putting two and two together and then making inquiries that could lead to the apartment she had rented.

The crisis arose late in the afternoon of the second day.

'Inquiries are being made for a person of your description,' Mocca had informed her gravely.

Amanda's heart rose to her mouth.

'Who is making the inquiries?'

'His name is Charles Arnold.'

That staggered Amanda. 'What?... How?'

'Does it worry you?'

'It's vaguely disturbing.'

It made no sense to her. Charles Arnold had no reason to pursue her. Surely petty malice didn't extend that far. Was Mr Complimentary Upgrade making use of that name to confuse her?

'The bodyguard can dispose of him,' Mocca said with satisfaction. 'We will throw him in the well from which no-one ever returns.'

'No, no, no,' Amanda said hastily. 'That's going too far. But it does mean we must leave Alcabab immediately.'

'All is not yet ready.'

'Then make it ready. We will leave tomorrow morning at three o'clock.'

'But everyone is asleep at that hour.'

'That's precisely why we're leaving at that time. Those who are too sleepy need not come.'

Mocca showed disapproval at such impetuosity, but did as he was bid.

They left the city only an hour and a half late. None was too sleepy to come. Mocca accompanied her. So did most of his uncles, brothers, cousins and others who laid claim to some more complicated relationship. As occasion necessitated, they were skilled truck drivers, mining engineers, explosive experts, camping specialists or generally useful for such a safari into the Atlas Mountains. What they did in real life, Amanda had no idea.

Wives came, as well. To do the cooking, Mocca explained. All their wages, of course, had already been invoiced to the palace. Mocca was riding on a sea of riches, the like of which had never come his way before. He clearly believed in making hay while the sun shone. Every night he prayed to Allah for more. The palace was as good as a money-machine, as good as owning the printing press itself. He seemed to have a permanent smile on his young face.

Amanda eyed him curiously as they began their long trek to the location marked on her father's map. 'How old are you, Mocca?'

'Seventeen, but nearly eighteen.'

'How is it that the older members of your family are happy to defer to you and take orders from you?'

His grin flashed very wide. With his mass of black curly hair, his unlined skin, his dancing dark eyes, he looked like a precocious, mischievous child who was far too knowing for the years that he had lived.

'It has always been recognised that I am the intelligent one in the family,' he boasted. 'Much has been expected. Now I have proved myself. I am no longer the boy. I am the man. I bring in the business. Ever since I was a little boy, I make more money than anyone else. This brings me much respect.'

It did everywhere in the world, Amanda reflected, yet she preferred the respect given to her by the one man who had all-seeing black eyes. He respected the person she was inside. She wished she could stop thinking about him. He disturbed her equanimity, her peace of mind, her composure... even the sense of duty which had driven her to resign her position as general manager of a first-class hotel.

She concentrated on watching the land unfold as they travelled on. Her father had passed this way many years before. He had headed towards the high plateaus. They were his undoing.

The Atlas mountain range traversed several north African countries, Morocco, Algeria, Tunisia... but here in Xabia, the geological formations were especially rich in minerals. Amanda imagined her father's excitement at being granted the chance to discover whatever he could find. With his intelligence, knowledge and endurance it would have been the highlight of his career.

He had found what he had been looking for in the ancient crystalline rock, but Xa Shiraq had turned on him, smashed his triumph, obliterated its existence from any known map.

One way or another, Amanda intended to redress that injustice. She was brooding over how it could be most effectively done when she saw a band of horsemen wearing black burnooses moving onto the road to block their route.

'Trouble?' she asked Mocca.

He shrugged. 'Members of the Chugah, the Berber tribe that inhabit this region. They are part of Jebel Haffa's personal troops. But we have the sheikh's permission to pass. There will be no trouble.'

Amanda hoped that was the case. The unsigned *chit* had worked like a dream so far. Yet the powerful name of Jebel Haffa sent a chill down her spine. He was Xa Shiraq's right-hand man. What if his troops had received orders to intercept the convoy and escort it back to Alcabab under guard?

The truck ground to a halt. The rows of horsemen parted to let through one lone rider on a magnificent white Arabian horse. He looked both majestic and intimidating in the black hooded cloak. Was it the Berber chieftain or Jebel Haffa himself? Amanda wondered anxiously. Another horseman broke ranks to follow him, holding his pace to the rear of his leader.

Mocca seemed to have no concern in confronting them. He alighted from the cabin, as brightly cheerful as ever, and waited beside the truck to greet the two men. The man on the white Arabian stallion did not dismount, nor did he make any acknowledgement of Mocca's greeting. He remained in his saddle, maintaining a haughty dignity as the second rider dismounted and conversed with Mocca in rapid Arabic.

Mocca broke away to come around the truck to where Amanda sat on the passenger side. She had the sheikh's note in her hand, ready to pass it to him but he did not ask for it.

'We are being honoured with a guide to take us through the mountain passes. He is to ride with us,' Mocca informed her.

'But we don't need a guide,' Amanda argued. 'I have precise maps of where I want to go.'

'It is not a matter of choice,' Mocca explained with an expressive shrug. 'It is a matter of honour.

They will be insulted if we refuse the offer. It is not wise to insult the Chugah. The guide is to ride with us.'

Amanda sighed, resigning herself to the customs of the country. 'Very well. If we must.'

There was a rustle of cloth, the squeak of the seat beside her. Amanda swung her head around from the passenger window to find their Berber guide already taking up the space between her and where Mocca would sit behind the driving wheel. She instinctively shrank away from the intruder, not because there was anything offensive about him but because she was suddenly assailed by the sense of some powerful alien force in his presence. It had happened to her once before quite recently.

Her nerve-ends jangled, even as she quickly reasoned that she was being absurdly fanciful. A guide was no more than a guide. She simply wasn't used to a hooded stranger in close proximity to herself, a big, hooded stranger whose face was obscured by the cowl and a masking cloth. Both were totally superfluous in the cabin of the truck where no dust was kicked up by horses' hooves.

The guide did not remove them. His arms were folded beneath his cloak, and his attention remained rigidly directed to the road ahead. He was totally immobile.

Most probably he was offended by her, Amanda assured herself. A bare-headed, bare-faced, foreign woman in jeans and shirt might be shaking his sense of propriety. They were a long way from the civilising influences of a capital city now, and the Berbers were born and bred mountain men.

Mocca swung into the driver's seat and closed his door, trapping the three of them into an awkward intimacy. Amanda steeled herself to get used to it and turned her gaze firmly forward. She was stunned to see the Berber spokesman leading the white Arabian stallion away, a riderless white Arabian stallion!

The back of her neck prickled.

Who was the man beside her? Why would the leader of these fighting troops belonging to Jebel Haffa appoint himself her guide? It was a lowly task that could have been undertaken by any of his men. How could any guide give directions to where she wanted to go if the guide did not know where she was going?

It only made sense if he was charged with more than guiding her. Amanda had told no-one exactly where they were heading. She had given Mocca only the most general instructions.

Mocca switched on the engine and the truck started to rumble forward again. The rest of the convoy followed suit. If everything went to plan they would be at their first camping site in the next hour or so.

Amanda concentrated on acting naturally as she put away Xa Shiraq's note and spread out her map of the area. Any deviation from the route marked by her father and she'd know for certain she had a problem.

A big problem.

CHAPTER SEVEN

THEY came to the wine village of Tirham in the Ozimi valley without further incident. Only then did their self-appointed guide break his stillness. He waved his hand and pointed to a junction side road.

'What does he want?' Amanda asked tersely. She was tired after travelling for twelve hours. Tirham was their destination for today and she certainly did not want to go any further.

'We must go where the guide points,' Mocca answered, resignation in his voice, and turning the truck onto a narrow road that led away from the village.

Amanda would have liked to argue the point, gave the inscrutable stranger next to her a quick glance, and decided against it.

'The villagers will be disappointed,' she reflected in courteous disapproval.

'True,' said Mocca, but he did not turn back.

Amanda was not so trusting. On the other hand, Mocca believed he had good reason to trust whereas she knew she was on borrowed time.

The man beside her was a disturbing enigma. Was he a deaf-mute? There had been absolutely no response from him to the spasmodic conversation between Mocca and herself. His presence had blighted the last hour.

As much as Amanda had tried to ignore the Berber leader, she had been unable to lessen her tense awareness of him, waiting for a movement, waiting for a word that might confirm her worst fears. She hoped Mocca was right and this detour was insignificant and meant nothing more than the end of today's journey.

They passed through a forest of magnificent cedar. At the dawn of civilisation cedar trees like these had flourished throughout the fertile crescent. They came to a cleared area beside a quickly flowing stream of sparkling water. A large, ornate tent and another group of silent, unmoving Berbers filled a small portion of the area.

Their guide tapped Mocca's shoulder and pointed to where Mocca should park the truck and those that followed. It was some fifty metres from the tent, the furthest possible distance away within the clearing. Some of the Berbers moved forward to direct the rest of the convoy to their corresponding places.

Amanda had the sinking feeling she had seen clockwork precision planning like this before. Who, she wondered, was in the tent?

Mocca hopped out to assert his position in this matter.

For the first time the enigmatic Berber guide turned his face towards Amanda. All was still hidden, but Amanda had the impression of the darkest sable eyes, deeply socketed, radiating energy and light. He waved his hand and the gesture was unmistakable. He wanted her to alight.

'I'm staying right here,' Amanda said, hoping the stranger understood English.

There was a shrug of the shoulders and the guide turned to the other side of the cabin and stepped out, Mocca deferentially holding the driver's door open for him. Without another sound or gesture, the Berber leader headed for the tent, his cloak billowing out behind his tall and imperious figure as his long strides ate up the short distance.

He paused at the entrance to the tent, turning slightly to one of the two men who seemed to be standing guard there. The man nodded as though he had been spoken to. Not a mute, Amanda deduced, her fears and suspicions growing stronger by the second.

She couldn't drive away. That would be admitting defeat. To run away would be to jeopardise her quest. Besides, if this was, indeed, the long arm of Xa Shiraq reaching out to gather her in, she doubted there would be any way to escape. Better to sit tight and wait to see what happened next. Tomorrow she would insist on having her own way and see if that produced any result.

The black cloaked figure moved inside the tent and disappeared from her view. The man who had received his instructions moved to meet up with Mocca and converse with him. Both men then turned and came to the truck where Amanda still waited.

'You are invited to take refreshments while the camp is being set up. There are more comforts for you inside the tent,' Mocca informed her. He smiled infectiously. 'It is also necessary. There is no other way.'

Neatly arranged, Amanda thought, certain now she was dealing with Jebel Haffa himself, the most loyal of Xa Shiraq's lieutenants. Her business in Xabia would be discussed privately in his tent. The decision of how to deal with her might have already been made. She might never get to Xa Shiraq. Nor to the crystal caves in the mountains.

'Get my bodyguard,' Amanda directed Mocca.

'There is no need. We are under protection,' he excused.

'Some bodyguards they turned out to be,' Amanda scoffed. 'The first time I need them, they evaporate like water under the midday sun. You can reimburse the palace for them, Mocca.'

He gestured an eloquent appeal for forbearance. 'They will be at your service, if service is required. But this is a matter of hospitality, not hostility.'

Amanda knew all about complimentary hospitality, as masterminded by Jebel Haffa. With a sense of fatalism, she picked up her bag and stepped down from the truck. The least she could do was conduct herself with dignity. Her heart was pounding painfully but she would show no hesitation, no fear, no faltering. She had come to right an injustice. She would be heard, if nothing else.

The Berber guard escorted her to the tent and gestured for her to enter. She felt the trap closing around her as she stepped inside and the door flap behind her was lowered into place, ensuring complete seclusion from Mocca and his extended family.

Richly patterned carpets had been laid on the ground. The aroma of freshly brewed coffee wafted on the air. But there was a stronger scent permeating the interior of the tent, a fresh, beautiful scent she had never smelled the exact likeness of before. It was tantalising, making it difficult to concentrate on the proceedings that were about to take place.

It was intensely discomfiting to find only one man waiting for her, the man in the black burnoose who had sat beside her in the truck. For the past hour he had known this moment was coming, ignoring whatever transpired between Mocca and herself because he knew all he had to do was ensure they took the road to this tent. When had he laid his plans...this morning after she had left the city?

He stood beside the table where the coffee and plates of sweet biscuits and fruit were waiting. He waved an invitation to the chair that had been set for her...opposite his. It was not a camp chair, any more than the table was a camp table, set as it was with an embroidered linen cloth. The backs of the chairs were ornately carved, the seats cushioned and upholstered in burgundy brocade. This tent and its contents marked his status as a very important person.

Amanda decided not to speak until she was spoken to. There was no profit in saying anything until the situation was clarified. She moved to the chair indicated and sat down. He walked to the other end of the tent where there was a large divan bed covered with the same burgundy silk as on the chairs. A group of plump, decorative cushions were piled on top of it. Her host obviously didn't believe in sleeping rough.

Outside the tent music began to play. Amanda wondered if this was to be the entertainment. She identified a violin, flute, tambourine, and possibly a guitar.

What was the scent teasing her nose? It seemed to be sharpening all her senses ... or was she confusing it with the very real sense of danger that was making her feel more acutely aware of herself and everything else? Especially the man who was now discarding his burnoose, tossing it negligently on the bed.

He swung around to face her and Amanda's stomach contracted as though absorbing a physical blow. She stared at him, her mind cartwheeling through a dizzying series of logical steps that brought home the realisation she could never achieve what she had set out to achieve. Not in the way she had planned it. Xa Shiraq and his men had been one step ahead of her, all the way.

And this man ... who would have been her lover if she had allowed it ... this man who had pursued her from Fisa ... this man who could command the Chugah, Jebel Haffa's personal troops ... could she still *touch* him ... sway him from his loyalty to the sheikh?

He stood absolutely motionless, watching her re-action to him with those all-knowing, all-seeing black eyes. She should have known, in the truck, who he was. Her instincts had told her. Neither cloak nor cowl could smother the innate power of the man. She had never met his like before their encounter at Fisa. It had been blindly stupid of her not to link the same force with the same source.

Not that it would have changed anything, Amanda assured herself. He would have engin-eered this result regardless of any effort she might have made to change it. This was his territory. Without an army to fight his troops, Amanda could not have evaded him. Tirham was the gateway to the mountains that held the crystal caves.

'You knew I would be coming here,' she stated flatly.

'Yes.'

'The promotion at Fisa was to see if I would be content with a career in hotel management.'

Again that flash of respect in his eyes. 'Yes.'

'The *cachet blanc* from Xa Shiraq...that also was a deliberate test of my purpose. To see how quickly I could think.'

'Yes.'

'Why was I allowed to come this far?'

'There is a saying in your country—"Give a person enough rope so they can hang themselves." You were given sufficient rope, Miss Buchanan.'

He paused to let her feel the noose tightening around her neck. Both ruthless and relentless, Amanda thought, with a little shiver of apprehension. As he had been with Charles Arnold, after giving him enough rope to damn himself.

They both knew he could have had her arrested at the embassy in Bejos for false representation of the sheikh's authority, but it would have been dealt with by officialdom in Bejos. Perhaps the fraudulent act might have been dismissed as a misdemeanour at that point. Not any longer.

'You wanted me in Xabia,' Amanda reasoned.

'It had a certain piquancy. Yes!'

'Revealing my intentions.'

'Beyond all reasonable doubt,' he affirmed.

'Putting myself in your power.' Would he use it to condemn her or rescue her? Did he still want her, or had she put herself beyond the pale as far as he was concerned?

'I arranged it that way,' he acknowledged.

'Under the jurisdiction of Xa Shiraq,' she mocked, reminding him he wasn't entirely his own man, hoping it might prick some deep core of pride that she could reach and use to her advantage.

There was a hard, unyielding look to his face. His black eyes bored into hers with merciless judgement. 'You cannot dispute you have broken the law. You made an illegal entry into this country. To that offence you have added the illegal acquisition of permits and goods that would be considered criminal acts in any country. You are guilty of so many counts of fraud and grand larceny, there is no international body you could appeal to that would interest itself in fighting your cause.'

'I have justice on my side,' Amanda bit out determinedly, refusing to accept the defeat he was pressing upon her.

His lips curled in contempt. '*Fiat justitia, ruat coelum*,' he said. 'Let justice be done though the heavens fall.'

'As you sow, so will you reap,' Amanda retorted.

He dismissed her words with a wave of his hand. 'You have discredited yourself in the eyes of the world.'

'The same ploy was used on my father.' She stood up in disdain of his indictment of her. Her eyes flashed their contempt back at him. 'Do you feel proud of your petty schemes and plotting?'

'It was efficient,' he stated coldly. 'And served its purpose. You are here in Xabia, Miss Buchanan. There is no avenue of escape.'

Was there no chink in his armour? Did he belong body and soul to his sheikh?

'That doesn't mean you win,' Amanda fired at him, trying to stir the sense of contest he had seemed interested in before.

It provoked him. The black eyes blazed, their chill obliterated by a heat that seared her skin. 'Time is on my side. As much time as I need. As much time as I want. You can hardly say I have lost, Miss Buchanan.'

Amanda was left in no doubt of what he meant. The arrogant confidence with which his eyes roved over her made her burn with furious resentment. It also triggered a flood of responses that shamed her.

Chemical reactions were uncontrollable, she reasoned wildly. There probably wasn't a woman in the world who wouldn't think he was over-whelmingly attractive in those form-fitting trousers and riding boots, outlining the strong muscularity of his legs and drawing attention to his virility. It was only natural that she should feel ... a tingle of interest.

Though, if she was honest with herself, it was more than that. Much more. She had the strong sensation of desire licking over her skin, sending curls of excitement through her stomach, down her legs. She found herself staring at his mouth, wanting it to ravish hers. She dragged her gaze down to his throat. The smooth polish of his bare skin in the V of his open-necked shirt incited a com-pelling urge to touch. She wanted to feel the power of the man enveloping her in physical intimacy, surging inside her, loving her for what she was.

Amanda struggled to come to terms with the strength of these feelings. It wasn't like her to have erotic thoughts. There was something else bothering her, as well. The scent ... it seemed heavier, richer now. But that was irrelevant to the problems she faced.

'I have had this tent prepared for you. For your comfort and pleasure.' His voice was suddenly a low velvet purr, a caress that squeezed her heart.

'What *is* that scent?' she blurted out. It was a stupid question, yet she somehow needed to have it settled and out of her mind.

'It is the scent of the jasmine that was banned by the Sultan of Zanzibar.' He walked towards her with the slow, threatening grace of a panther on the prowl, his black eyes gleaming with satisfaction. 'The Arabs complained that it unduly excited the women when they were having sexual relations. Personally, I don't mind that happening.'

Resentment welled over the strange excitement that had gripped her. 'Does having me as your prisoner give you the right to do anything you like with me? Is that what you think?'

'I will use whatever means I have to make you face the truth of your feelings as a woman. And your response to me as a man.'

'Does that include taking me whenever you want to?'

He laughed derisively. 'I want more than that.'

He was close now, so close that the compelling demand in his eyes made her feel intensely vulnerable. 'Do you have Xa Shiraq's approval for what you are doing?' she fired at him, desperate to find some weakness she could play on.

'If I risk that disapproval, it is for you.' His arms came around her waist, drawing her to him. His eyes burned into hers. 'What would you risk for me, Amanda?'

It was the first time he had taken the familiarity of using her name. It was seductive. It was also revealing. For all his steely control he was not immune to her. She still *touched* him...and troubled him...as no other woman had. That was what he had told her in Fisa. The critical question was how far would he go to have the complete conquest he wanted.

She pushed her hands up his chest to retain some distance between them. She barely resisted the impulse to explore further. She had to think, act, win!

'What do you want me to risk?' she asked.

'Yourself. Open yourself to me—your mind, your heart—in ways you never have before.'

'And you?' she whispered, spreading her fingers over the firmly delineated muscles of his chest, feeling them tighten under her touch. The primitive urge to claw, to hold the beat of his heart in her hands was incredibly strong. 'Would you do the same for me?'

'Yes,' he rasped.

But would he pay the price?

'Even if it means being disloyal to Xa Shiraq?'

CHAPTER EIGHT

AMANDA felt the brief suspension of his heartbeat beneath her palm. It stopped completely then resumed at a slower rate. Shock, followed by a clamp of control that amazed her with its swift and steady application. A shutter came down on his eyes, as well.

Mentally regrouping himself, Amanda surmised, and doubted this man would ever entirely lose himself in passion, no matter how deep or urgent or compelling the physical desire.

'Do I take a viper to my heart?' he mused. His hold on her slackened.

'You said you would open your mind to me,' she pressed, sliding her hands up to his shoulders, moving closer in desperate supplication, her eyes begging his for a stay in judgement. 'Have you never questioned Xa Shiraq's decisions? Might they not sometimes be wrong? Wrong about my father?'

She saw his eyes harden.

'You said you wanted to know my heart,' she argued. 'Well, I have loyalties, too, and they go as deeply as yours. How can I commit myself to you if you deny what I am?'

'You are mistaken,' he said flatly.

'How do you know? Does the sheikh tell you everything? Or do you carry out his orders with blind faith in his judgement?'

He stiffened, his pride stung. His eyes flared a warning. 'It is well that I had the musicians play to drown out all sound. You talk of disloyalty and treason...'

'I need a few days of freedom. That's all. You've let me come this far. Please...' her hand moved instinctively to touch the pulse at the base of his throat '...it means so much to me.'

His head jerked back. He pulled her hand away from him and stepped out of her reach, his eyes slashing her with fresh contempt. 'You seek to corrupt me with your body. I will not take it. Your price is too high.'

He swung on his heel and strode towards the bed, tall, straight-backed, bearing a supreme dignity in his incorruptibility. It struck a deep chord of respect in Amanda. How Xa Shiraq must value this man!

If only she could have him at her side...his strength of mind, his sense of integrity, the power of his spirit. Her heart clenched. She could not let him go, thinking so badly of her. It wasn't true. She had to make him see it wasn't true. Somehow that was far more important than proving her father right.

'How can it be anything more than bodies...when you deny me understanding?' she said quietly.

He stopped in the act of bending to retrieve the black burnoose. Slowly he straightened, his back still rigidly turned to her as he considered her words.

'I loved my father,' she pressed on, wanting him to realise it was a statement of fact, unshakable, enduring, an intrinsic part of her that he could not cut out.

'He is at rest now. It is best that you leave him there,' he said just as quietly, not without sympathy.

Relief poured through Amanda. She had *touched* him again. Encouraged, she asked, 'Would you, if it was your father?'

She saw his shoulders lift and fall as he breathed deeply and released some of his tension. He swung around to face her, an implacable look in his eyes.

'If there was good reason, yes,' he said with steely resolution.

'And I suppose Xa Shiraq gave you good reason for my father to be discredited,' she said with an acid bite. 'Making him out to be a liar when all the time he was a victim of your sheikh's chicanery.'

He grimaced. 'Xa Shiraq does not expect you to see the matter in the same way he does.'

'For years I lived with the need to clear my father's name. Do you expect me to forget it all in a minute on your word that it is best that I do?'

He made no reply.

'Tell me the good reason!' she demanded.

He shook his head.

'Why not?'

'You know not what you ask.'

'So you decide for me,' she mocked. 'Where is the sharing of minds and hearts in that?'

'There are matters of far greater consequence than you,' he snapped.

She ignored that and advanced on him, adrenaline running high, determined on *touching* him again. 'All the time in the world will not win my trust if you won't give me yours. Or is it your plan simply to dominate me, and keep yourself apart?'

For the first time she saw conflict in his eyes, a dark raging turbulence that coalesced into one searing need. 'I am tired of being without a true companion.'

'So am I,' she whispered, her heart turning over at the vulnerability he revealed.

He stepped forward and scooped her hard against him. She felt a tremor run through him at the full impact of their bodies coming together. There was a quiver inside herself, as though of something momentous being recognised.

'You,' he murmured, his eyes burning into hers, probing her mind and heart and soul with an intensity that pierced any possible deception. 'You could be the price that cost a sheikhdom.'

He lifted a hand to her cheek, his fingers stroking her skin as though needing to draw absolute truth from her. 'Show me what you promise,' he commanded.

Then his fingers raked through her hair to grasp her head and hold it to his as he kissed her.

If that was what it could be called.

Certainly his mouth claimed hers and ravished it with an invasion so passionately intense, Amanda was totally lost in the bombardment of sensation, drowning, yet connected to a source of vibrant energy that thrummed through her body, a surging river of it, stirring an overwhelming compulsion to stay linked to him.

Yet it was not a subjugation. While she had the sense of falling into him, she felt him falling into her. Her arms curled around his neck, her hands cupped his head, holding him to her, and she felt strong and invigorated, and soft and melting all at the same time.

There was no remaining aloof from what was happening. It was captivating, enthralling, touching deep hidden places that rejoiced and savoured being drawn from isolation, suppressed no longer, released and winging free from the cage of loneliness, soaring and swooping from one to the other in jubilant recognition of finding at last there was somewhere else to belong...welcomed...wanted.

She was barely aware of his mouth leaving hers, of her head dropping onto his shoulder, cradled there against the warm strength of his neck. Her mind was intoxicated with dreams of what could be possible, her body safe in the warm haven of his arms. She felt him breathe and her own lungs filled. He sighed and she knew it was the wind of change.

She felt the ripple of new energy through his body, the stirring of purpose, control firming, but she did not believe he could retreat from her now. Physically yes, but not mentally, not emotionally, not spiritually. If he did, it would be a violation of something so precious it would be akin to homicide.

'Amanda...' There was both awe and pain in his voice.

So strange, she mused. He had not even given her his name. She tried *Jebel* in her mind. It didn't quite fit the deep dark strains of power in him...the elemental primitive man that called to all that was untamed in her.

'You would come to me...of your own free will?' he asked.

The strained note in his voice told her he wanted to believe it, but his intelligence questioned it. She wanted him to let her go free. She wanted her father exonerated. The stakes were high.

'Yes,' she said, not knowing where this would end, no longer caring.

However it had happened, an act of destiny or pure accident, Amanda was sure in her own mind that there would be no other man for her. Why it should be, she didn't know. The perversity of fate was imponderable. A collision course had been set, and once effected, there was no going back.

She felt the quickening of his pulse. He eased back from her, lifting his hands to cup her face, draw her gaze to his. He looked into her eyes and she didn't mind him seeing the desire for him openly reflected there. She was sorry to see the torment of uncertainties in his.

'I will put an end to this matter. You are tired after your long journey. Perhaps distraught. I should let you rest. I should not have pressed so hard. For all your inner strength . . . you remain a woman.'

It was a strange, tortured mixture of concern and tenderness and self-criticism. It was as though, having hunted, he was struck by an empathy with his prey, and he could not bring himself to move in for the kill.

'Was *more* too much?' she asked with rueful irony.

'No. You both humble and exalt me.' His hands glided slowly, gently, down her throat to her shoulders. 'I will leave you now. I will send you a serving woman who will see to your needs. I will not have you sleeping in the company of herdsmen and goat keepers. There is no reason for you not to accept the comforts I can provide. It is all for you.'

He stepped back, picked up his burnoose. With a whirl of black cloth it settled around his shoulders and he strode away from her, heading for the door.

'Where are you going?' she called after him.

He paused, looked back. 'To contemplate the oddity of human foolishness. Including my own.'

'Where will you sleep?'

'Under the stars.' His lips quirked into a self-mocking smile. 'They have been my companions for a long time.'

'What about tomorrow?'

'It will come.'

'Will you be here?'

'Yes. Whatever happens . . . whatever is decided . . . you are now under my protection. We are linked...you and I. Though much can come between us, and probably will, the link is irreversible, is it not?'

'Yes.'

'Are we damned by that knowledge...or blessed with it?' he mused.

'I don't know,' she murmured, aching to go to him, yet accepting that he must work through his own quandary of spirit. 'Are you Jebel Haffa?' she asked, wanting to put a name to him.

He seemed to consider the question far longer than was necessary. 'Jebel Haffa is loyal beyond all price,' he answered enigmatically. 'His loyalty is legendary and goes beyond that of any figure who has lived through history.'

He reflected for a moment and continued. 'He is part of me. The part that is rational and far-seeing. The part that executes what needs to be done for the good of the people of Xabia. But there is another part of me that is not Jebel Haffa.'

The part I touch, Amanda thought. The personal side.

'It is the part of me that has journeyed through the long years alone, in a void of emptiness that was never filled no matter what I did or how much was achieved.' His eyes glittered derisively at her. 'Was it worth it?'

'Of course,' she protested.

'When you have all the answers to the questions about your father, what will be the worth of it, Amanda? Will you end up holding an empty goblet in your hand, with nothing left in it to drink?'

A chill ran down her spine. Was she chasing a rainbow that had no substance to it?

'I've been there before you,' he said quietly, sadly. 'One strives for the goal, but when it is reached, the satisfaction never lasts. It is so brief. Ephemeral. And afterwards, one looks back...and counts the cost. It is all too easy not to think about the cost...until afterwards.'

'You're saying that my quest is futile and I should give it up now?'

He shook his head. 'I know it is futile but until you are aware of it, you will not give it up. Cannot. Therefore I must set my course accordingly.'

He lifted the black cowl over his head and turned to leave.

'Wait!' she cried. 'I don't want you to pay a price for me. I take back what I asked of you. It wasn't fair. I had no right.'

His head swung back towards her. His black eyes burned like live coals in the shadow of the cowl. 'Don't you know, Amanda?' he said softly. 'There is always a price to pay for everything. There is a price you and I will both pay. It is written in the stars. It is inescapable.'

He left her with that remorseless thought.

The scent of the Xabian jasmine drifted back into her nostrils, reminding her of all the needs of a woman. She didn't know why tears came to her eyes, why they kept welling up and trickling down her cheeks. Human foolishness.

She had won something, hadn't she?

Yet there was no sense of triumph. Not even satisfaction.

She was alone. And cold. And the memory of her father had somehow lost the power to spark the fire in her belly. Another man did that. The man, almost certainly, used by Xa Shiraq to shame, damage and humiliate her father.

CHAPTER NINE

HE WAS outside the tent when Amanda emerged the next morning. He was alone. Clearly no one else was allowed within the vicinity.

His face was rendered indistinguishable by the cowl of his burnoose, but now Amanda would have known him anywhere. In any clothing.

She felt his eyes snap over her in quick appraisal. Amazingly she had slept well. Perhaps the jasmine scent also had soporific qualities. The early morning air was crisp, engendering a sense of vitality, but *he* added dynamism to it. Amanda waited for him to speak, aware that her fate lay in his hands.

'You are ready to depart now?' he asked without preamble.

It was the authoritative part of him that spoke. No desire. No intimacy. Cool, decisive, distant. His night under the stars seemed to have brushed aside the part of him he had revealed the previous evening. Perhaps disloyalty to Xa Shiraq sat uncomfortably on his shoulders. Perhaps much depended on her attitude this morning.

Was he waiting to discover which way she would turn? Was he watching like a cat to see how the mouse would try to avoid the danger and traps which abounded?

Amanda had decided last night he was not Jebel Haffa. The roundabout way he had answered her question about his identity inclined her to believe he was a far more complex man than the faithful follower Jebel Haffa was purported to be, probably someone higher in authority who worked behind the scenes. That fitted the anonymity he was intent on keeping. It also fitted what had happened at the hotel in Fisa.

'I'm ready for any new challenges,' she answered calmly. In her mind she added, *Mr Complimentary Upgrade*.

'You will instruct Mocca to lead your convoy on to the location marked on your father's map.'

Amanda could not hide her surprise. 'You know about that?' For years she had considered the maps her secret weapon.

'Your father was hardly discreet. You are not the first to come looking for Patrick Buchanan's great discovery,' he said dryly. 'It is as well to have another failure, particularly by his daughter's expedition.'

He was so confident it would fail. Had her father been mistaken? Amanda couldn't believe it. Even in the delirium preceding his death by pneumonia, her father had still been lucid about the crystal caves. They had to exist.

'You're allowing me to continue?' she asked, wary of misunderstanding his intentions.

'Your convoy will follow your exact instructions in everything. They will go, they will search, they will not find what you are looking for.'

'Where will I be in the meantime?'

'With me.'

It was a flat statement of fact, not allowing her any choice in the matter. It gave her no indication of what they would be doing together.

He nodded towards the camp where Mocca and his extended family were bustling around, packing up, ready to depart. There seemed to be far more efficient organisation in their activities this morning. 'Go and give your orders. Then you will return here to me.'

It was clear she was to appear to be a free agent, although she wasn't. If she deviated in any way from his instructions, Amanda had the sinking sensation that her fall into disgrace and oblivion was virtually certain. She resigned herself to doing what was requested and set off to speak to Mocca, determined that both her manner and words be above criticism.

She had no idea if Upgrade's reference to being partly Jebel Haffa was significant or merely symbolic. Whatever and whoever he was, he was still acting under orders from Xa Shiraq. It seemed highly unlikely that these arrangements were his own. Although he probably had some latitude in carrying out the sheikh's will.

She hoped his manner would be different once they were alone. *If they were to be alone*. How she had got herself into this situation, and how she was going to get herself out of it, Amanda did not precisely know.

She might be about to be whisked off to Alcabab to face justice according to Xa Shiraq. She might be accused of treason against the State.

On the other hand, if she were to rejoin Mocca at the site to be explored, and that exploration did prove to be an exercise in futility, the sheikh could consider her failure as the definitive means to bury the question of Patrick Buchanan's discovery once and for all. In which case, why wasn't she being allowed to go to the site and confirm the failure?

If he wanted her expedition to fail in a blaze of publicity she would be accompanying it. As neither of these situations seemed feasible, it meant one thing with certainty. There was a deeper purpose behind what was happening.

Excitement tripped her heart into a faster beat. If Upgrade had wanted her simply for his pleasure, he could have had her last night. He had chosen differently. Perhaps his words revealed not so much desire and wanting and vulnerability, but instead constituted an excuse to withdraw.

Amanda had the disturbing feeling that she was nothing but a pawn. If that was the case, Amanda knew enough about chess to know that pawns could become queens. She hoped to show Upgrade how it was done.

'Good morning, Miss Buchanan,' Mocca greeted her in singsong triumph. His grin was very wide. 'You see? There was no...o...o problem. Your bodyguard would have been an insult to your great patron.'

'Who is my great patron, Mocca? What is his name?'

Mocca shrugged. 'Many words are whispered, but none can tell. Some things it is better not to know.'

'Well, my great patron has invited me to stay with him while you get on with my business, Mocca. I guess it wouldn't be wise of me to make a daring escape.'

Mocca shuddered. 'Forbid the thought. To so blatantly refuse hospitality could cost us all our lives.' He rolled his eyes for emphasis. 'You are highly honoured, Miss Buchanan.'

The honour was highly questionable as far as Amanda was concerned.

Mocca pondered a moment. 'The camping equipment I bought for you was not good enough.' He gestured towards the tent. 'My eyes have been opened. I did not foresee the will of Xa Shiraq to the proper degree.' He smiled infectiously. 'Trust me, Miss Buchanan. I am the brains of the family. Next time I do better. My third cousin twice removed is an importer of camping equipment.'

'I'm sure he is,' Amanda said dryly. 'Now this is what I want you to do...'

Mocca listened attentively to her instructions. He repeated them back to her word for word. He volubly assured her that all would be ready for her, when she was ready.

In the meantime they would do a preliminary search for the caves, although they were not to enter them without her.

Maybe he would collect more supplies. He would purchase a special tent for her. For someone who held a *cachet blanc* from the Sheikh of Xabia, nothing was too much trouble.

Amanda thought of her list of crimes as outlined by Upgrade. She firmly instructed Mocca to spend nothing more. He was simply to do what he had been told.

She handed the map to the Berber who was to accompany Mocca. He was the spokesman of yesterday. She suspected he would keep Mocca's natural bent towards excesses under direct and strict control.

The far more important map remained in her bag. She had not been asked for it and she wasn't about to hand it over. Other people might have scouted the general area where her father had made his discovery. Amanda refused to believe they could have had a duplicate of the precious map that marked the exact location of the caves. She might yet be able to turn the tables on Xa Shiraq. All she needed was the opportunity. Then seize it.

She had promised her father on his deathbed she would do her best to remedy the injury he had sustained. She had not considered the possibility that there could be good reason not to. Did that invalidate a deathbed promise?

Amanda felt less certain than she had for years. Her sense of purpose was being eroded. She was deeply troubled as she walked back to where Upgrade was waiting for her. He had said yesterday there was much that could come between them. It was probably already in place. He would have put it there.

Horses had been brought into the clearing. He stood beside his white Arabian stallion. Next to it was a beautiful black mare. Her luggage, which had been brought into the tent by the serving woman, was now loaded onto a packhorse. The mounted troops formed a guard of honour by the road back to the village.

Her serving woman was standing by, a black burnoose draped over her arm and a pair of riding boots in her hands. Amanda had no trouble in deducing she was going on a journey which would begin on horseback. She exchanged her Reeboks for the boots without a murmur of disagreement.

'How did you know I could ride?' she asked, turning to the man who had the power to change her life.

'It was a recreation you partook in at the Fisa hotel,' he replied, moving to help her mount the black mare.

'Where are we going?'

'To do my will.'

That was the very information she needed. Not Xa Shiraq's will. *His* will! It didn't precisely tell her where they were going but she now definitely knew whose *will* was taking her there.

'I don't like not being consulted,' she said, trying out a small challenge.

'You will see for yourself that it was far better that you were not consulted,' he replied with frustrating equanimity.

She shot him a brooding look. 'I don't like you one bit when you get into this all-knowing mood.'

He ignored the contentious comment.

Amanda wondered if there was anything he didn't know about her. She knew nothing of him. His life was a complete mystery to her. What of his family? Where had he come from? When had he first become allied to Xa Shiraq? What was their connection to each other? Surely this journey must provide her with some answers.

Once she was in the saddle, he set about adjusting her stirrups so she would ride more comfortably. It seemed wrong to her, this leader of men, carrying out such a task while his troops watched and waited.

'Should you be doing this?' she asked, acutely aware of the interest and attention being directed at them.

He paused and looked up, the black eyes burning from the shadow of his cowl. 'That which is precious must be pampered. I would not allow any other man to touch you.'

Heat raced through Amanda's veins. It was virtually a claim of possession in this country. *His* woman. Was that why he had sat between her and Mocca in the truck yesterday, isolated her in the tent last night? As sternly as he was standing back from her this morning, she was most certainly under his personal protection.

He took the black burnoose from the serving woman and handed it up to Amanda. 'Put this on,' he commanded, 'so that idle eyes will not note our progress once we leave.'

He didn't explain why idle eyes could be a problem. Amanda wondered if it was to hide her from other men's vision. On second thoughts, she realised the burnoose was purely practical if Mr Complimentary Upgrade was going against Xa Shiraq's will.

Amanda watched him swing himself into the saddle on the white stallion. He was so lithe, supple, strong, graceful. A little quiver of anticipation fluttered through her stomach. He was a man worth having. It might be incredibly primitive, but she secretly revelled in the idea of being claimed by him. Claimed and possessed.

He nudged his horse forward with his knees. Amanda's black mare needed no urging. The moment the white stallion moved, the mare followed, ready to fall into place beside it.

That was natural, Amanda thought. It had always been so.

The Berber horsemen formed a cavalcade, some riding ahead of them, most behind, both groups far enough away to allow private conversation between herself and the man beside her.

They did not stay on the road to the village. They struck out on a trail through the cedar forest, bypassing the village altogether. She heard the drone of the convoy's engines fall further and further behind them. At a signal from her companion, the Berber troops departed. The white stallion was reined in to a prancing halt. The black mare simply stopped.

'What happens now?' Amanda asked.

'We strike off into the mountains on our own. We will ride hard and fast. I will not spare you.'

He paused to reflect a moment. 'You asked for my trust. I give it.' He looked at her with hard unyielding eyes. 'I hope you are worthy of it. The price of betrayal is death.'

It sent a quiver of fear down Amanda's spine. Was he speaking of his betrayal in not following the sheikh's orders, or the vengeance he would wreak on her if she betrayed his trust?

Amanda quickly gave him her assurance. 'I will not betray you.'

'And the cock crowed three times,' he said sardonically.

It was a wretched feeling, being torn two ways, Amanda reflected. She wondered if she would end up betraying the promise she'd made to her father. 'I'm sorry you feel that,' she said quietly.

The soft words seemed to spur him on. 'We are now set on the path that leads to either heaven or hell. There is no in-between. There is no going back. Unless you do so now. You can say goodbye and we will never meet again. You can link up with the convoy as it passes through the village of Tirham. Make your choice.'

His inner tension reached across to her, squeezing her heart. She knew intuitively he was playing the biggest gamble of his life. What that gamble was she could only guess at. She had no doubt he wanted her with him, wanted her to prove her mettle, yet there was this hesitation within him, perhaps because she was a woman and he considered any woman softer, weaker than himself.

She remembered the way he had withdrawn from her in the tent, observing that she was *a woman*. And this morning he had remained aloof, pressing nothing except organisational commands. Had he deliberately refrained from applying any emotional influence so that she could freely make the decision he now offered her?

It affronted Amanda.

'How could any woman resist your entreaties when they are put in such endearing terms?' she mocked at him. 'Of course my decision must be to go with you.'

Once again there was a flash of compelling respect in his eyes. It was a look Amanda would have gone to the grave for. All her miserable existence as the butt of jokes dissolved into a nonentity of the past. To earn the respect of such a man as this squashed every cruel malicious word spoken by Charles Arnold and others of that ilk.

She looked at the strong ageless face, saw the loneliness behind it, and knew she was not alone. The yearning for a true companion was sufficient to take any risk.

'I'll go on with you,' she repeated simply.

'So be it,' he answered.

She caught a brief raw blaze of desire before he turned his head forward. Amanda's heart began a wild pumping. She had taken the plunge. It should be fear she was feeling, she thought, but it wasn't. It was excitement.

She wondered what manner of man she was dealing with, who could offer her heaven or hell—whatever one or the other or both would be like—then ride on towards it with a bold hand on the rein of her horse.

If she wanted to let her mare gallop, she had to loosen the bridle. That was the thought uppermost in her mind.

Then she wondered about herself. That she could make the choice so easily...and ride with him...wherever he cared to take her.

CHAPTER TEN

AMANDA was determined not to wilt. By late afternoon it was sheer willpower that kept her in the saddle.

They had ridden hard and fast. She was certainly not spared. The mountain trails were rough and became narrower and narrower. There was no such thing as an easy walk, let alone a canter. Galloping, thank heaven, was too dangerous to attempt on this terrain.

Every bone in her body was jolted. Every muscle screamed in protest. It was just as well that the black mare followed the white stallion without any urging. Amanda was reduced to hanging on. How much further? she longed to ask, but pride would not allow her any confession of weakness.

When they'd stopped for lunch, hours ago, she had still felt fine. The morning ride had been a lot faster but not nearly so arduous. They had emerged from the forest to slopes that were terraced for agriculture. There were apricot and apple orchards, fig and olive trees. It had been quite pleasant, climbing to the high pastures which were dotted with flocks of sheep.

That was all behind them now. Scattered stands of green oak and juniper trees grew between outcrops of bare rock, but vegetation was sparse this far up amongst crumbling gullies and limestone ledges. Amanda was in no state to appreciate the scenery anyway. She figured she was going through the hell part of the path they were set upon, and the heaven part had better make up for it.

At last they came to a resting place. It was like an oasis in a mountain desert. For a few moments, Amanda wondered if she was hallucinating. She blinked several times but the natural rock-pool was still there. So was a glade of pine trees and grazing grass for the horses.

'We'll camp here for the night.'

It was a welcome announcement. The only problem was, Amanda didn't think she had strength enough to get off her horse. She watched Upgrade dismount with an easy fluid action. His legs weren't seized up. His arms weren't limp.

Mind over matter, she sternly advised herself.

It didn't help. The messages from her brain simply didn't penetrate to her booted feet. They remained stuck in the stirrups. She did manage to unclench her fingers from the reins and grab hold of the pommel of her saddle.

'I'm afraid I'm incapable of moving,' she declared ruefully. 'I've never been riding this long. It's not that I'm weak,' she argued. 'I'm simply all used up.'

She didn't realise the words came out slurred. She thought they were very precise and her logic was perfectly reasonable.

Amanda wasn't quite sure how he got her off the horse but his arm around her waist certainly as-

sisted. She was glad he didn't try to set her on her
feet because she had the feeling her knees would
buckle. It felt extremely comforting to be cradled
securely in his arms. He carried her some distance
and laid her gently on the grass.

'I'll be back in a minute,' he said.

'Mmmh,' she answered, overwhelmed with
fatigue.

She closed her eyes and let herself float above
the aches and pains. She felt her riding boots being
eased off her feet and vaguely thought that was a
good idea. Loosen up her toes. Her jeans were
another matter. When he unfastened them and
started pulling them down, Amanda jolted out of
her daze of exhaustion. Undressing her to that
extent was distinctly inappropriate. She was in no
condition to feel or respond to anything.

'Not yet,' she mumbled.

'I'm going to massage your legs with liniment.'

'Sensible,' she agreed, relieved that nothing was
expected of her.

He had wonderful hands. Wonderful liniment.
It spread tingling heat deep into her muscles. Or
so it seemed. Amanda thought she could take a lot
of what he was doing to her. Her legs were be-
ginning to feel as though they belonged to her again.

When he started working on her toes, there were
definitely messages working up through her body
to her brain. Squirmy, exciting, little messages. She
had read somewhere that women could have or-
gasms from having their toes fondled. She thought
it would be interesting to check it out.

'I'll do your back now.'

With that assurance, Amanda saw no reason to resist being further undressed. He unfastened the burnoose, unbuttoned her shirt, lifted her a little to draw the sleeves from her arms, then gently rolled her onto a rug that he must have fetched from one of the packhorses.

He covered her legs, keeping them warm, then removed her bra and swept her hair aside. She still had her panties on and she had lain on many a beach like this, so there was really nothing to feel self-conscious about. The fact that she was alone with a man halfway up the Atlas Mountains didn't change anything. He was the right man.

Besides, he was being very professional, like a nurse, and it was undoubtedly for her own good. His slow, deep, controlled breathing indicated nothing. Nevertheless, she couldn't help wondering how much he liked what he saw, how really physically appealing she was to him, whether touching her was pleasurable, exciting...and where it would stop. If it did.

He moved to kneel astride her, his knees pinning the rug on either side of her thighs. Amanda's eyes were closed but the image of him poised directly over her supine body burned into her mind, stirring an exquisite sensitivity to his touch. It wasn't until he had worked over her back and shoulder muscles for some time that Amanda could relax completely and simply let the soothing motion flow through her.

She drifted off into a sensual dream where she was floating on a gentle sea and delicious waves rolled around her bottom, making her feel especially soft, buoyant and feminine. Then utter oblivion swallowed the dream and she was aware of nothing until she awoke to a range of little noises; horses snuffling, the crackle and spit of a camp fire burning, the soft crunch of footsteps.

She became conscious of other things. She was warmly and softly cocooned in a sleeping bag, a makeshift pillow under her head. It was dark. The sky was ablaze with stars. There was the smell of coffee with a touch of cloves. Her body, when she moved it, was slightly stiff in the joints, but no longer aching. She turned herself slowly towards the sounds and the smell.

He was crouched beside the fire, his body still cloaked in the burnoose, but with the hood thrown back. The flickering light threw his profile into sharp relief. Again she thought he had the kind of strong, noble face that was struck on ancient coins. Its ageless quality suggested an endurance that could suffer and rise above any adversity. Indomitable.

She wondered about his origins. He didn't look Arabic. The Berbers were a Caucasian race, but he didn't look like one of them, either. Perhaps, he was simply unique to himself and that set him apart, contributing to his loneliness.

He was still holding himself apart from her despite the need he had revealed, despite her willingness to embrace the man he was and go with him wherever he led. Was he having second thoughts? Did her collapse after the long ride diminish her in his eyes?

She wished she could tell what he was thinking... feeling. She wished she had woken up in his arms. She was sure that the physical contact would have reduced everything to simpler, more basic terms. Her body tingled with the memory of his hands moving over her bared flesh. He already knew her far more intimately than she knew him. If she called to him now...

'Have I slept long?' she asked.

He wasn't startled by her voice. He turned his head to look at her, his face gathering shadows that made his expression indecipherable. 'It is almost dawn. We must leave soon.'

His voice was quiet, calm, decisive. So much for any thought of making love! This man was not about to be tempted from the course set in his mind. His air of relentless, ruthless purpose was not softened or mitigated in any way.

Amanda felt decidedly frustrated. She was both surprised and chagrined to find she had slept a good eight hours, the night was virtually over, and she was none the wiser about Mr Complimentary Upgrade apart from the fact of him being a superb masseur.

She suddenly realised her stomach felt very empty. 'I need food,' she said bluntly, wary of the pace he had set yesterday and the need to restore a high energy level.

'We will eat as soon as you have washed and dressed. You will find fresh clothes beside you.'

The thought of another day's riding made Amanda quail inside. 'Aren't the horses tired?' It was the only excuse she could think of that might allow her more rest.

'They are. They are also mountain bred. They will not let fatigue hold us up.'

Amanda sighed. A petulant stand was out of the question. She would lose his respect. She had made her choice, accepted his conditions, and it ill behove her not to continue with as good a grace as she could muster. Particularly since he was looking after her aches and pains and feeding her as best he could.

He was organised and efficient. By the time Amanda had finished breakfast, the camp fire was doused and scattered into non-existence, everything was packed up, the horses were saddled, and there was no trace left behind of their night's sojourn here. Amanda wondered if he was still concerned about idle eyes. Or was he expecting Xa Shiraq to have them tracked once it was realised they were no longer with the convoy?

The sky was lightening as he helped her mount the black mare. Her bottom settled gingerly on the contours of the saddle. Amanda decided, on behalf of the torture her muscles were anticipating, that one small challenge was in order.

'I think it's only fair you should tell me how far we're going today so I can get myself mentally prepared for it. After all, a marathon runner knows he only has to pace himself through twenty-six miles, three hundred and eighty-five yards. How many yards do I need to pace myself through?' she added dryly.

'Many,' he said.

'Thanks for the precision,' Amanda rejoined.

He pointed to the highest point of the mountain range they were traversing. 'That is our destination. If you can steel yourself to the journey, we should make it there in good time.'

In good time for what? she wondered. 'Does it have a name?'

'In Arabic it is called the Gemini Peak.'

'Does it have a twin?'

'To the north. Where your convoy is going to. We cannot view it from here,' he said dismissively.

Amanda's grey cells hit turbo assist as they went into overdrive. Pieces of the puzzle left by her father slotted neatly into place with those few words from Mr Complimentary Upgrade. A twin peak to the one her father had described!

No wonder her father's discovery had been discredited. No wonder that no one else had been able to refind the caves her father had spoken of. They were being directed to the wrong mountain top!

Every map, including the precious one she had so carefully kept to herself, positioned the crystal caves on the peak to the north of the wine village of Tirham. Its *twin* peak, to the south, was not entered on any map Amanda had seen. The omission had to be deliberate and her father somehow misled about direction. That was why Xa Shiraq's duplicity had lain unrevealed for so long.

Upgrade knew the answer to it all. He was betraying his sheikh to show her the secret. It explained the restraint he had forced upon himself, no matter how pressing or urgent the desire he felt for her. First, he would give her what she wanted, what she had come to achieve. Only after that was accomplished would he come to her as her lover. Only when he had given all he had to give.

It touched Amanda deeply. When the time came, she would repay this man with all the love and affection and tenderness in her heart. What he was doing for her was a sacrifice of heroic proportions. Her instinctive reactions to him had been so right.

He had already mounted. She urged the black mare up beside the white stallion before he set off. 'Come what may,' she said with renewed determination, 'I will ride with you this day. I will not fail you. I will not falter. I'll be with you at the end.'

His stygian black eyes gleamed their approval. 'That is how it should be,' he said simply. He turned his horse's head, and led off into the blaze of glory as the sun crested the mountain ridges with its mantle of fire.

Amanda found it impossible to estimate the distance they had to cover. It was reassuring to know where the termination point was. Bubbles of adrenaline spurred her on. What had once appeared so unattainable was now within reach.

The thrill of knowing that her father, now dead, could figuratively hold his head high in pride diminished the jolting, bruising ride. There was a sense of purpose in the gruelling journey, although she still didn't know what the end result would be.

She pondered further on the problem as they rode steadily upwards. Perhaps the Gemini Peak marked the border between Xabia and another country. Furthermore, it might be a safe route for her out of Xa Shiraq's grasp.

Considering the crimes listed against her, Amanda realised that Upgrade could be rescuing her from a lengthy term of highly unpleasant imprisonment, as well as saving his own skin from retribution. It made sense of the speed he pressed on her, and the need to avoid any possible witnesses to their passage into these mountains.

Amanda was not keen on running away. Not if she actually found the crystal caves. It nagged at her mind. Would Upgrade be happy as an exile to a country he had served with great personal commitment? Would she be happy knowing her mission to establish the truth of her father's discovery was aborted without full restitution being made? Could anyone ever scuttle all that had made up their past lives?

Amanda felt as rootless as her father had been. She had a conviction that some things were worth fighting for. Like justice. And fair play. Her instincts told her it would be better for both her and Upgrade if they faced up to Xa Shiraq.

The problem lay in whether Upgrade would agree to it or not. Could she rescue him from Xa Shiraq's wrath by playing her cards right, forcing a stand-off so that Upgrade didn't have to face exile? Power could be challenged with power. Firstly, she would have to re-establish contact with Mocca, then get to her embassy. Amanda had a lot of faith in Mocca's resourcefulness.

Once that had been done, and she had her own government's support, she would beard Xa Shiraq in his den. There were ways and means of establishing a truce once she had her bargaining tool.

As plans revolved around Amanda's mind, she started taking more notice of landmarks along the trail they travelled. She might have to go back alone if Upgrade rejected her ideas. He would follow her. She had no doubt of that. However, she might very well need a head start to accomplish what she wanted.

The day wore on. They didn't stop. A water canteen and a bag of dried fruit and biscuits were attached to Amanda's saddle. She didn't starve and she didn't die of thirst but the long exhausting ride took its toll. She was almost reeling with fatigue when a halt was finally called beside a small rocky mountain stream that trickled down from the peak.

'This is far enough. We leave the horses here.'

The black mare came to a stop next to the white stallion.

'Why?' Amanda asked. The peak looked so close now. Enticingly close. 'Surely an hour or two more....'

'The horses cannot go where we will go. This is the best place for them to rest.'

'You mean we are to continue on foot?'

'Exactly.'

'So we save the horses and kill ourselves,' she said with an attempt at ironic humour.

'You cannot go on?' he asked, his dark eyes scanning hers in concern.

'Where you go, so, too, will I,' she said loftily.

'Good,' he approved, taking her at her word.

Nevertheless, he helped her off the mare and gave her some time to wash her hands and splash her face with the cold water from the stream while he saw to the horses, unsaddling and tethering them. She did her best to collect a second wind as she watched him swing a pack on his shoulders, ready to trek forward.

He didn't say anything. Neither did she. He took her hand in his, and strode off without a backward glance.

They climbed.

He assisted her, supported her, pushed her. Amanda went on like an automaton, beyond fatigue, holding on, moving one foot after the other. They came to a ledge which was blocked by a monstrous stone.

'It's no good,' Amanda said. 'We can't go past it or get around it.'

Upgrade took no notice of her. He dropped the pack from his shoulders, unbuckled it and took out two hydraulic jacks.

'I will lift the rock sufficiently for us to bypass it.'

He suited his actions to his words. Curiosity drew Amanda forward to observe. The rock had been cut at the base on either side, but one side much higher than the other in order to take the jacks.

Upgrade manoeuvred them into place, then started the lifting process. One side was kept at the same level to form a fulcrum on which to lever the other.

Amanda watched in fascination as millimeter by millimeter the great block began to tilt. It revealed a small crevice set into the rock wall.

'You will crawl through that.'

Amanda looked incredulously at Upgrade. He had to be joking.

He waved her forward. He wasn't joking.

Amanda did as she was told with deep trepidation. What if the great block slipped off the jacks? The thought of entombment sent spears of horror through her. She tried to calm herself with the assurance that at least she wouldn't be alone. He followed her into the narrow space, pushing her towards an impenetrable darkness.

She could feel her throat choking up. She thought of *Aida*. How the two lovers had sung together after their entombment was beyond belief. That was opera. This was real life.

Then there was no rock constricting her passage. She swept her arm around to make sure. There was nothing in touching distance. Very cautiously she rose to her feet and stepped forward into a sense of timeless, eerie space.

She heard Upgrade straighten up behind her. Then there was a click and in the glow of torchlight she saw for the first time what her father had discovered.

Only then did she understand why it had haunted him for the rest of his life!

CHAPTER ELEVEN

THE illumination refracted from thousands of millions of facets of the crystal lining the cave, protruding from the walls in flower-like shapes, feathering down from the roof. It was like a magical fairyland, sparkling with ancient mystery and the promise of riches beyond belief.

It was entrancing, enthralling, and as the torch swung in an arc, it magnified the effect of being encased in a fantastic prism that bathed them in glittering rainbows. It was all her father had described. More. The memory of it must have been burned into his mind...an inescapable torment, impossible to forget.

Tears welled into Amanda's eyes. To have the enormity of this discovery suppressed and disbelieved when he knew all along he had seen what she was seeing now... 'It's true,' she whispered in an agony of apology for the doubts that had sometimes clouded her faith in his claims about the neodymite crystal caves. 'All true.'

She turned blindly to the man who had brought her here, instinctively reaching out to him in the darkness behind the torch. 'I can't tell you how much it means...'

Her heart was so full she could not find the words to express all she felt. She stumbled forward and half fell against him. His arms swept around her, holding her to the strong, warm solidity of his body. She couldn't help it. She wept, overwhelmed by this resolution to years of striving . . . trying to console her father, trying to bolster his cause with her belief, trying to work her way to proving the truth, once and for all.

'Thank you,' she choked out. 'Thank you for doing this for me.'

'No man could have asked more of a daughter,' he said softly. 'Your father has a right to be justly proud of you.'

'But I'd never have found it without you.'

'You had an unquenchable belief. Such beliefs move mountains. You would have found it, or lost your life striving for the unattainable. I merely took it into my head to save yours.'

'You've been here before. You must have been.'

'Once.'

'Before the entrance was sealed?'

'Yes.'

'Why did you decide to share it with me?'

The hand on her hair moved to her face, feather-light fingertips caressing her cheek. 'Would I be a true companion to you if I let you suffer the pain of never knowing what you wanted and needed to know?'

His lips brushed her fringe aside and pressed a kiss on her forehead. 'I want your mind to be at rest.'

His hand dropped to the soft swell of her breasts. 'I want your heart to be content.'

His body moved more intimately against hers. 'I want you to be at peace with yourself, and with me.'

Amanda was transfixed by the beautiful simplicity of his words, the sweet transmission of giving implicit in his touch. It rippled through her body, washing away the lassitude of deep fatigue, stirring anew the deep womanly needs that called out to be mated with this man.

She felt his physical response, the hardening thrust of his flesh against hers, the sense and urgency of his youth pulsing from him, reaching out to her, wanting. Her mind danced with a wild singing of yes...oh, yes, I want you...yes...and her heart took up the refrain with a rapid tattoo of affirmation.

He expelled a deep sigh and turned away from the tempting contact, his arm curling around her shoulders to hold her close to his side as he moved forward. 'I will show you all there is to see,' he murmured, his voice strained with the necessity to complete the task.

He was right, Amanda thought with a heartfelt rush of gratitude. This place belonged to her father. They were walking now where he had been before them, their feet crunching on orbs of crystal that had broken away and shattered on the rock floor. This was one of the great natural mineral repositories of the world...and the justification of her father's belief in himself.

'It's magic,' she whispered, as strange shapes loomed up ahead, some fluorescing under the light of the torch, others taking on the appearance of transfigured images. 'How far does it go?'

'There are many caves.'

'All like this?'

'Some smaller, some larger.'

She thought it strange that the air did not smell musty. Perhaps she was intoxicated by the sheer splendour of light reflected into myriad fascinating fantasies by the crystals. Perhaps the crystals freshened the air.

Or maybe she was light-headed from the excitement coursing through her at the continual brushing of her body against his, thighs, hips, the nestling of her shoulder under his arm. It made her feel small, feminine, protected. He hugged her more firmly whenever she stumbled.

The caves were interlinked, apparently honeycombing a considerable part of the peak. She knew they were looking at untold wealth and could well imagine her father's elation at having found one of the greatest treasures in the world. As a geologist he would have been in seventh heaven. Yet he had ended up in a personal hell.

Her feet faltered to a halt. 'I've seen enough for today.'

'As you will,' came the quiet rejoinder. 'There is always tomorrow.'

Amanda felt drained of the energy that had kept her going. All this had brought her father long-lasting misery. What had been done to him was unforgivably wrong. Her sense of injustice swelled as they started retracing their steps.

'Why was my father's discovery discredited?' It was a painful cry of protest. 'Why was the existence of the neodymite crystals suppressed?'

'You realise it's used as a catalyst in the manufacture of rocket fuel and other chemical processes?'

'Yes.'

'Your father refused to comprehend the consequences of what he had found,' came the quiet and unemotional reply.

'I don't understand,' she pleaded. 'There is a vast wealth for your country here.'

'I see death and destruction.'

'It could be used for good...'

'Don't be naive, Amanda.' His voice hardened.

'Whoever controls the source of neodymite controls the future,' she expostulated.

'Do you imagine any of the world's great powers would care what happened to Xabia and its people while they fought for their share of what is here?'

'Mining the crystals could be managed for the benefit of the people,' she insisted, not wanting to accept his dark view of inevitable consequences.

'Xabia will not become another Kuwait,' he went on remorselessly. 'Neodymite crystals are more valuable than the black gold that motivates war. There would also be the price of corruption.'

The cold certainty in his voice dampened her ardour for argument. 'Yet it cannot forever remain a secret.'

'No geologist will ever be allowed to venture into this area again. Every trace of this discovery has been expunged from the records. It will remain so.'

It stirred a fierce resentment in Amanda. 'You have no idea what that did to my father.'

'Your father was blindly obsessed. He would not see the danger.'

'He was an orphan. A homeless, Irish orphan. The butt of cruel jokes. You wouldn't know what it's like to be put down,' she said heatedly, smarting from the memory of all her recent treatment from Charles Arnold.

'We must all rise above such things.'

'Dad wanted recognition. Nothing more. It would have made him worth something to himself,' she defended. 'Xa Shiraq killed that in him.'

'Xa Shiraq was right, Amanda,' came the remorseless reply. 'Your father was wrong.'

'Not in my view,' Amanda said fiercely. 'Not by my standards. Xa Shiraq wasn't prepared to reach for the stars.'

She was stepping forward as she spoke. He stopped. His arm dropped from her shoulders. Amanda hesitated, glanced back. He stood absolutely still, a dark and suddenly menacing figure. The atmosphere in the cave seemed to thicken. She sensed turbulent emotion coursing through him, emotion that focused on her with frightening force.

Before she could do or say anything to appease it, he stepped forward, and played the torch once more over the cavern of crystal about them.

'What do you see, Amanda?' he demanded harshly. 'Fame and fortune? Is that what you crave?'

'No,' she cried in protest.

'Does your father's greed run in your blood, too?'

'It wasn't greed!'

'Power is very seductive . . .'

'It's not so,' she denied vehemently.

'Look at them. Millions of neodymite crystals twinkling their temptation. Beautiful and deadly. For thousands of years they have glittered unseen, storing up energy, waiting to shower it upon the world. Do they whisper to you to release it?'

It was strange. What she had initially seen as a magical fairyland now seemed to glint coldly, malignantly. She shivered. He pulled her against him, her shoulder blades meeting the firm masculinity of his broad chest, her bottom crushed to rocklike thighs.

'Xabia is prosperous,' he stated bitingly. 'There are no beggars in the streets of Alcabab. We have schools. We have hospitals. The people are not in want. Of what benefit are more riches, Amanda?'

She didn't know the facts well enough to dispute what he claimed. To speak out of ignorance could only earn his contempt. It was true what he said about the capital city. It had been surprisingly clean and orderly compared to other cities she had visited in the Middle East. Even the enterprising Mocca and his extended family had no complaint about their lot in life.

'As for the stars,' he continued mockingly. 'Isn't the space above our planet already filling with the debris of our rocketships? Why should mankind interfere with the stars? They have been more constant companions to me than anyone else. Leave them alone, I say.'

Amanda's heart sank. She had failed him. He had gambled on her seeing things his way, gambled she would give up her quest in favour of a greater wisdom. He had opened his mind to her and instead of sharing his perceptions, she had clung to her father's cause.

Amanda closed her eyes to her father's lost treasure and felt the pained thump of the heart behind her. 'I'm sorry,' she whispered. 'I've lived with this secret ... for so long ... to put everything right ...'

'The decision is now yours, Amanda. To reveal or not to reveal. That is the choice I have given you.'

Her father was dead. He was beyond hurting any more. It tore at her heart. To admit he had been wrong in pursuing what had been forbidden him was unthinkable. Yet ...

'Success and failure,' she whispered, 'both at the same time.'

'I have known it often.'

She believed this enigma of a man. The crystal caves belonged to the people of Xabia. Yet they could not use them. It was the paradox of life.

She would not take it upon herself to change anything for them. To right the injustice to her father was to wrong others. Let justice be done though the heavens fall, he had said with grim irony.

She would not let the heavens fall.

'Amanda...' It was both a demand and a growl of need, dispensing with choice as he turned her in his arms and tilted her face to his.

His mouth claimed hers before she could utter a word.

The swift infusion of his passionate energy dispelled the limp feeling of defeat. It smashed the tormenting spectre of a promise that would not now be fulfilled. It stamped another promise into her mind that seduced all reason, then into her heart, allowing room for nothing else but the stampeding pulse of togetherness.

Take me, his kiss said. *There is no fame or fortune or power in the world that could compensate for what would be lost if you choose another path*.

He reforged the link between them with tempestuous fire, welding the softness of her body to the burning rigidity of his, his hands sliding over her in pressure patterns that secured a fierce and intimate contact. He was rampant male, compelling submission to his will, yet inducing a yielding that exulted in his forcefulness, and the yielding brought its own harvest of response from him.

She felt the straining of his muscles, the tremor of need that rippled through him, the pounding of his heart, the endless thirst for her giving of herself to him. He had waited, restrained himself to breaking point, but now the floodgates of wanting were cast open and a torrent of desire swept all before it.

'Does this make up your mind?' he demanded hoarsely, his breathing as tortured as hers between kisses. 'Tell me it does. Give yourself to me.'

'Not here,' she pleaded, her voice raw with her need for him, yet the thought of the crystals surrounding them—her father's crystals—was abhorrent to her at a moment which should be clean of the past.

'This is not the place for us,' he agreed.

He swept her along with him, Amanda's feet barely touching the ground. He virtually carried her through the shimmering kaleidoscope of caves, back the way they had come, unerring in his sense of direction, urgency driving his every step.

Amanda was riven by her desire to go with him wherever he led. The knowledge she was leaving her father's dreams forever behind her was submerged. It had to be so, she told herself. She had her own life to live. The choice was made. There *was* good reason for letting things be as they had been for time immemorial. Her father had been the disturbing influence. This was her final farewell to him. She hoped he would understand.

They reached the entrance to the tunnel that led out to the pure mountain air, to a clear vista of the country so loved by the man who would be her lover, to a future she couldn't yet envisage, but it was waiting out there for her.

'Go ahead,' he urged as she knelt to crawl through to the crevice in the rock-face. 'I will follow in a minute. There is something I must do for you first.'

She couldn't imagine what it might be, but she didn't protest or linger. She hated the claustrophobic feeling of the narrow passageway and manoeuvred herself through it with driven haste, emerging on the open cliff ledge with an intense sense of relief.

She didn't touch the hydraulic jack near her feet. She was certain afterwards she did not. The weight it was supporting must have caused an overload in its mechanism. There was a loud crunch. The huge block of stone started to tilt towards her.

The shock of it robbed her of any wits at all. The instinct for survival must have taken over, forcing her feet to scramble out of harm's way. It was only when the massive stone rocked into its resting place, sealing the exit from the crystal caves that she began to scream, the horror of it bursting through her mind, clawing at her heart.

If he had not been crushed to death, he was sealed inside the caves...entombed with no way out. In irrational panic she rushed at the monstrous rock, tried to free the crushed hydraulic jack, tried to push the massive weight aside. She wept, she sobbed, she called out to him again and again.

There was no answer. Not a sound issued from the mountain to assure her she was heard, that all was well with him.

Dead, she thought numbly.

Finally it dawned on her that she had to go for help. She had to leave him and find people who could rescue him if he was alive to be rescued. If an arm had been pinioned under that great weight... Amanda shuddered in horror at the mental image. She had to get help before it was too late.

The secret of the crystal caves could not be allowed to be a secret any longer. She couldn't let him die in there. She wouldn't let him die in there. Whatever it cost, she would get him out.

CHAPTER TWELVE

Amanda slid, fell, stumbled, scrambled and hurtled down the narrow paths and slopes on the way back to where they had left the horses. Scratches, scrapes, grazes and bruises meant nothing to her. Heedless of any damage she might sustain, her mind was set on one goal and one goal only. Despair and desperation drove her on.

Wearied beyond belief, she made it back to their base camp before sunset. She could not afford the luxury of sleep. Once she closed her eyes it might be a day before she opened them again. There was only one thing she could do. She had to go on.

At least coming down the paths and trails had been far easier and faster than going up. She hoped that would hold true for the journey she had to make on horseback.

She tried to saddle the white Arabian stallion, reasoning he could go faster than the black mare. He wouldn't let her near him. She fell back on the mare, frantic to keep moving.

She hauled her battered body into the saddle. She tried knees, hands, reins, everything she could think of, but the mare only circled around, refusing to go anywhere without its mate.

Amanda cursed like an Arab caravan overseer. She cursed as she had never cursed before. Finally she managed to untether the white stallion and slapped it hard on its rump. It reared high on its back legs. Finally, and by good luck only, it took off along the trail by which they had come.

The black mare quickly raced onto its heels. Amanda knew she had no control over where they went, how they went, and the speed at which it was accomplished. She could only pray the white stallion would lead them to the nearest habitation so she could beg for a rescue party. If she could make herself understood.

They descended helter-skelter and Amanda felt sorry for her horse, obsessively intent on keeping up with the riderless stallion in front of them. It wasn't fair on the mare, but the mare didn't seem to care that she was carrying Amanda's weight.

Amanda understood the instinct that wouldn't let the female be parted from her male. Wasn't that why she was pushing herself beyond any rational limits of endurance to keep going?

She could hardly bear to think of what it must be like to be imprisoned in those caves. Was there a fresh supply of air creeping in from a crack somewhere? Was it enough to last for... however long it took to bring help?

How powerful were the batteries in the torch? If he was plunged into utter darkness... Amanda shuddered.

Hold on... hold on... hold on...

She did so herself.

I'll come back for you, her heart said, forever and always.

The mindless refrains of holding on, forever and always, helped to detach herself from the exhaustion enveloping her. She was no longer in control. The sheer mechanics of riding kept her in the saddle. She was oblivious to where she was, how far she had come.

The light was fading. She didn't know what she would do once night fell. Would the horses keep going? Was it wise to risk it? She had to!

Had to... had to...

She was numb, numb all over when she heard the helicopter. She had to concentrate hard on focusing her eyes, turning her gaze to the sky. It was too high, too far away for any occupant to spot her. She doubted she could find the energy to lift her arms to wave anyway. Futile effort. The helicopter went out of her line of vision without deviating from its course.

Despair dragged at her heart. She tried to pick out the landmarks she had taken note of earlier in the day. She thought she recognised a couple but had no real idea what they meant in relation to how far she had travelled from the Gemini Peak. The light was going fast now. She had no choice but to trust the horses to take her where she needed to go.

She remembered that in the days of Genghis Khan messengers had been tied to the saddle. She wished she had taken the same precautions. If she stopped, dismounted, she suspected the black mare would take off with the white stallion and leave her alone.

Impossible to contemplate such an outcome.

She caught herself reeling and forced herself to sit upright again. Darkness nearly on her. Have to stay awake, she told herself. She twisted the reins around her wrists, a warning tug if she should start to fall off. Sound of the helicopter again. No use to her. She didn't bother looking for it this time. No energy for that. It couldn't land here.

Darkness. At least she had the stars as her companions. She had to ensure he would see them again. The link between them couldn't be broken. Their togetherness was written in the stars. He had told her so. She believed him.

Body sagging. Rolling in the saddle. If she could rest for a moment. Close her eyes. So hard to keep them open. Just for one moment. Mustn't fall off...

A shout snapped her awake. She had slumped across the horse's mane. She dragged herself up. The mare slowed to a tired walk. Amanda couldn't see the white stallion. There was the drumming sound of hooves clattering towards her. Someone coming. Voices. She had found help. At last!

That thought was enough to sustain her wretched body, stirring it to an awareness of pain. None of it mattered. Only the message she had to deliver mattered.

Other horses steamed and stamped around her. Berbers talking across her in Arabic, taking the reins from her hands. She didn't have the strength to resist. She grabbed the pommel of the saddle to steady herself.

'Stop! Listen!' she cried. 'Does anyone speak English?'

'You will come with us,' one of them replied.

'No.' Amanda shook her head dizzily. 'I need help. We have to go back. To the Gemini Peak. Up there a man is trapped in one of the caves.'

'There is no order but the order of Xa Shiraq. You will come with us,' came the inflexible reply.

'But the man will die.'

'Undoubtedly. In the meantime, you will come with us.'

'No, I won't,' Amanda yelled hysterically.

Her plea fell on deaf ears. 'It is not a matter of choice,' she was told. 'You will go to the helicopter.'

Through the dizzying waves of fatigue, Amanda grasped one thing clearly. Using a helicopter to transport her bespoke power. 'By whose order?' she asked.

'It is the order of Jebel Haffa, who fulfils the will of Xa Shiraq.'

'These are the men I must see,' Amanda said, trying to drive conviction into her voice. 'I will use their power to have my way. Take me to the helicopter.' She hoped the words sounded as brave as the ideas behind them were.

Her horse was urged forward. The Berber riders were beside her, behind her, in front of her. She no longer had the reins. There was no room to dismount even if she mustered the strength to do so. She was comprehensively trapped by the escort.

'How long will this take?' she begged in utter desperation.

'Our orders are that we are not to be swayed by anything you say,' came the flat, relentless reply. 'We must not listen to any words you speak.'

'Oh, that's really great,' Amanda grumbled, frustration eating into her courageous facade.

She closed her eyes, silently and bitterly cursing Xa Shiraq. He must have found out she was no longer with Mocca and the convoy. He must realise he had been betrayed by the man now entombed inside the Gemini Peak. Xa Shiraq had entrusted that man with the task of seeing she never confirmed her father's discovery. Now her impossible task was to convince Xa Shiraq to go to the help of his betrayer.

The helicopter had probably been searching for them when she had seen it pass overhead. It was certainly no coincidence that it had been sent to this area. Xa Shiraq had been checking out the worst scenario he could think of and he'd come up trumps.

'Where is the helicopter going to take me?' she asked, hoping for some enlightenment.

'To the sheikh's palace at Alcabab.'

The vision of Mocca's invoices to the palace rose in Amanda's mind.

'Will I see Xa Shiraq himself?' she asked, keeping her tone light to hide the despair she felt.

The Berber shrugged. 'It will be as he wills.'

It was hardly a conclusive reply. Nevertheless, it did make sense that Xa Shiraq would want to question her. She wondered if he would order a public trial for her crimes. Unlikely, she decided.

He wouldn't want her blabbing about the crystal caves to all and sundry in an open court. Amanda was only too well aware of how much trouble he had taken to hide their existence. She would be spirited away, never to be seen again.

Yet she would surely get the chance to talk to him face-to-face. She would tell him all, plead with him, appeal to his finer senses of humanity. She would convince him to rescue the man who had served him loyally and faithfully for so many years.

Or would Xa Shiraq leave the man to die miserably of thirst and starvation in the deep black vaults of the crystal caves?

'Help me off this horse,' she demanded when the troup of cavalry halted at the helicopter. Bravado seemed to be her best recourse in this situation.

'No.' It was the Berber captain who spoke.

'How am I to get off it then?' she asked.

'Fall off it,' he prompted unsympathetically.

'Why won't you help?'

'It is forbidden to all men to touch you,' he said.

Amanda swore again in the most unladylike manner. In her present condition there was no way she could maintain any dignity without assistance. If this was a deliberate act of humiliation...

'Let me get this straight,' she said in biting anger. 'You are not to listen to any words I speak, you are to say as little as possible to me, and you're not to touch me.'

'That is correct,' came the unemotional reply. 'That is the order of Jebel Haffa to the will of Xa Shiraq.'

Amanda gritted her teeth. Words were useless weapons. She was faced with brick wall adherence to orders. If she was to get to Xa Shiraq, she had to make it to the helicopter by herself.

Somehow she managed to slide herself around the neck of the horse. It galled her that she presented anything but a dainty picture. The Berber men looked on expressionlessly as she eventually staggered onto her feet at ground level.

Amanda was more riled than she had ever been in her whole life. She was being treated as an outcast. A pariah. Purdah in its cruellest form! She felt the steam level of her boiler rising.

'Take me to Xa Shiraq,' she demanded. 'I'm going to give him a fair whopping piece of my mind!'

CHAPTER THIRTEEN

KOZIM found it very stressful when Xa Shiraq
maintained silence for longer than five minutes.
Kozim found it so stressful that he timed Xa
Shiraq's silences so he could be quite sure whether
to feel stressed or not stressed.

What was even more stressful was when Xa
Shiraq accompanied the lack of speech with the
tapping of his fingers. It meant the sheikh's mind
was working in mysterious ways that would inevitably confuse him. Kozim could then lose respect
by giving the wrong answers.

Xa Shiraq's respect meant a great deal to Kozim.
Indeed, it was imperative he keep it. To Kozim, it
was the most important thing in his life.

He decided a safe comment was in order to
prompt the sheikh into talking again. This would
almost certainly diminish the build-up of stress.

'I had all the trash cans in the sheikhdom intimately examined and scrutinised,' he said.

The black eyes focused on him with nerve-tingling
intensity. 'Why did you do that?' The voice gave
no indication of approval or criticism.

The question spread uncertainty through Kozim's
mind. 'I wondered if a rare jewel might be found.'

The fingers tapped again. 'Did you find any
jewels, Kozim?'

'No, Your Excellency.'

'Don't bother doing that again.'

'Of course not,' Kozim said miserably. 'Most unfortunate.'

'The geologist's daughter requires attention, Kozim.'

'I thought it would come to this,' Kozim said quickly. 'Will I block payment of the bills?'

Xa Shiraq's mouth curled sardonically. 'No. Mocca has an extensive family. It behoves us to give an occasional boon to such people. From such matters, legends are born.'

Kozim blinked. It was extraordinary how Xa Shiraq knew everything. Even the least significant of his people in Alcabab did not escape his attention.

'Fire must be fought with fire,' came the grim announcement.

'That's so wise,' Kozim hurried to agree.

'The woman has gone too far.'

'Women always do.'

'Entombing people goes beyond good-natured fun.'

'Absolutely.'

'It calls for the most severe retribution.'

Kozim had some expertise in the field of retribution. 'Beheading was a favorite device of the British monarchy for many centuries. Henry the Eighth had a certain natural flair...'

'I need worse,' Xa Shiraq growled. His fingers tapped a particularly strong rhythm.

'The unspeakable or the unmentionable?' Kozim asked. 'Which do you prefer?'

'Both!' Xa Shiraq said decisively. 'She should suffer both!'

'Wise,' said Kozim. 'You are not only esteemed, respected and loved for the qualities of mercy and justice, but, oh, so very wise.'

Kozim glanced quickly at Xa Shiraq. The deadly resolve in those all-knowing black eyes made him shudder. Once more he reflected how glad he was that he was not the geologist's daughter.

CHAPTER FOURTEEN

As soon as the helicopter landed in the palace grounds a swarm of women came forward to help Amanda. They lifted her into a richly ornate sedan chair that could have been commissioned by an empress of Rome. Although she welcomed the softly piled comfort of silk and satin cushions after the rigours she had been through, it was a painful reminder that the man she had left behind had nothing but cold, hard stone to lie on.

No-one would listen to anything she said. The women were as deaf as the Berber men to her pleas, to logical argument, to any compassionate understanding of the situation. They were unswervingly persistent in following their own schedule and Amanda simply didn't have the strength to resist the ministrations that followed her arrival in what had to be the sheikh's harem.

She was stripped with gentle but firm efficiency, pushed and pressured into a spa pool and thoroughly lathered and washed as though she were a baby. In truth, she felt as helpless as one. Her hair was shampooed and brushed dry. Her thoroughly cleansed body was massaged with some wonderfully soothing body lotion.

Her guilt at accepting such treatment was appeased by the thought that it had to be against all protocol to be presented to the sheikh looking the way she had. Fighting this process would only cause more delay in getting to Xa Shiraq. But it was agony thinking of what might be happening up in the crystal caves.

She was clothed in a simple gown of white silk. She was urged into eating a thick creamy soup. It seemed sensible to comply since she couldn't afford to be weak from hunger. The soup was delicious and filling. Her tastebuds told her it was a mixture of seafood. As she ate, the drowsier she became.

She awoke in a luxurious bedchamber, lying between satin sheets, and it was broad daylight. A woman attendant smiled benevolently at her. Amanda wanted to scream and rant and rave at the appalling passage of time that represented untold suffering for the man she had to save.

'How do I get to Xa Shiraq from here?' she demanded, with little hope the woman would understand.

She didn't. Or pretended not to. She made a swift exit from the bedchamber and before Amanda could swing her feet to the lushly carpeted floor, a whole team of twittering servants poured into the room to start the pampering all over again.

Amanda kept repeating the name of Xa Shiraq to no effect whatsoever. The women insisted she dress in a long-sleeved caftan-style gown. It was black and reminded her of the burnoose that she hoped was providing some warmth for Upgrade if he was still alive.

She went into rebellion. She couldn't, wouldn't eat anything from the platter of exotic fruits provided for her breakfast. She wouldn't drink her coffee. She searched for a way out of the harem. There was none that she could find quickly.

In anguished frustration she cried again, 'I must get to Xa Shiraq. I have to see him. Please...can somebody help?'

A reply came from the oldest woman in attendance. 'A messenger was sent that you are rested and well, Princess.'

'How long will it be before I'm granted an audience?' Amanda demanded, ignoring the odd form of address to her.

The woman shrugged. 'It may be a day, perhaps a week, a month or two...who can tell the will of Xa Shiraq?'

'I can't wait that long!' Amanda protested. 'I have to talk to Xa Shiraq within the hour.'

A gong resounded from somewhere close. The women burst into excited twittering. The older one who had answered Amanda in English moved to the locked door at the far end of the room and opened a peephole. There was a quick exchange of Arabic. The woman turned to address Amanda.

'The time has come. An escort awaits to lead you to the sheikh.'

Amanda barely stopped herself from running to the door. It was unlocked and opened for her before she reached it, but a few more seconds weren't about to make any difference. She knew she had to control her seething impatience. It was paramount that she impress Xa Shiraq with reasonable behaviour or he would undoubtedly scorn anything she had to say.

The escort of four men was in ceremonial military dress. They marched along on either side of her. It looked like a guard of honour, but Amanda had no delusions about that. She wondered if it was supposed to lull her into a false sense of confidence before the axe dropped on her neck. Xa Shiraq certainly had no reason to welcome her presence in his country, let alone his palace.

She fretted over how best to beg his mercy, whether any approach at all would soften his heart or appeal to some generosity of spirit. She was totally blind to the beautiful works of art she passed in the corridors on her way to him; splendid mosaic murals, exquisite urns, ancient carvings, all testaments to a cultural heritage that was proudly displayed and cared for. She thought only of what she had to accomplish and the ways and means to accomplish it.

Her mind flitted over many explanations that would justify Upgrade's betrayal to his sheikh. None satisfied her. She doubted Xa Shiraq would comprehend an emotional link that went beyond rationality.

The paired escort in front of her came to a halt at a double set of huge doors. With well-trained timing they opened them and stood back for Amanda to enter the room ahead of her by herself. As she had anticipated, it was no open court filled with people. It looked like a private library, the walls lined with books, the furniture comprising highly polished desks, leather armchairs, reading lamps.

Her gaze quickly swept the room as she stepped inside. She tried desperately to quell the nervousness and apprehension that threatened to reduce her to a jittery and hopelessly inadequate advocate for her cause. She was determined that none of what she really felt would show on her face or in her body language. If anything, she wanted to project defiance.

There were two men present, only two to confront and convince, she told herself in an attempt to minimise the mountainous problem facing her. While they looked intimidating in their official Arab robes and headdresses, Amanda steeled herself to think of them as ordinary human minds she could bend her way.

The one rising from the chair behind his desk was short and stout. The other, apparently perusing the book in his hands, was turned away from her but Amanda instantly identified him as the sheikh by the gold and black twisted 'iqal that held his headdress in place.

He was a tall, formidable figure, and Amanda felt her stomach knot with apprehension as she heard the doors close behind her. An overwhelming sense of force and power emanated from him, holding her captive, yet he made no movement, gave no sign of acknowledgement that she had intruded on his consciousness.

She'd experienced this before.

Twice before.

Her heart clenched in painful yearning for the man who had made her feel so much. He had to be alive. If only he were here, Amanda was sure he could meet Xa Shiraq's power with an equal strength that would have commanded respect. She had to act in a manner worthy of him.

The sheikh read on, ignoring her presence, or pretending to, perhaps waiting to see if she would crack, perhaps silently expressing contempt for her.

There was a waiting stillness about him that accelerated her heartbeat to a painful tempo. It reminded her of the stillness of the man who might at this moment be still for a more deadly reason.

She darted a glance at Xa Shiraq's associate and was startled to find she recognised him. It was Mr Kozim, the man who had handed her the page telling of her promotion to general manager of the Fisa hotel.

A spark of hope kindled in Amanda's heart. Surely he would be sympathetic to an appeal for the life of a man he had worked closely with, even though his first allegiance was to Xa Shiraq. Mr Kozim definitely had an air of stress about him. He cleared his throat with a nervous little cough.

'Your Excellency, the...uh...geologist's daughter is here.'

Amanda had no doubt the Sheikh of Xabia was aware of that. He was letting her stew, wanting to unnerve her. What was more, he was succeeding. She could feel his wish to torture her with his silence, to keep her on tenterhooks until she snapped into an outburst that he would use against her.

She grasped at the straw that Mr Kozim represented and did her best to turn the situation to her advantage.

'Mr Kozim, you are a man of great understanding and humanity,' she appealed, not knowing if he was or not, but a little flattery could not go astray. 'I appeal to you on behalf of the man who carried the orders of Jebel Haffa at the Oasis Hotel at Fisa. I ask you to intervene on his behalf to Xa Shiraq himself.'

Mr Kozim's face went pale. His hands fluttered nervously along the desk. He coughed. 'You do not know what you ask,' he said in a strangulated voice.

Not much help there, Amanda thought, and her eyes swung away from him so they would not reveal her despair.

She said no more. She grimly held her tongue, determined to outplay the sheikh in this contest of wills. She knew instinctively she would win nothing by grovelling. She had to convince him that the crystal caves meant nothing to her. Only then might he listen to her appeal to free the man who had gone against his will.

Amanda had the sinking feeling that few people went against Xa Shiraq's will without suffering horrendous consequences. She had to quickly decide on her course of action.

Any lack of control on her part would raise suspicions about the reliability of the promises she would give him. A man such as he would only respect strength. She must show that strength and let nothing daunt her.

She straightened her shoulders more rigidly than they had even been set before. She turned to face him square on. She took one step forward to draw his attention, then stopped. She would go no further until he gave his response.

The book in his hands was slowly clapped shut. It was replaced in the empty slot on the shelf behind him. Amanda felt her chest constricting as he started to turn towards her. Her mind jammed with desperate prayers.

His profile came into view and shock hit her like a sledgehammer, completely smashing all her fiercely held resolutions.

'You!'

The cry burst from her lips in a released avalanche of pent-up tension and frustration, combined with all the pain and bitter suffering that had tormented her waking hours since she had last been with him.

Blazing black eyes scorched over her with scathing contempt. 'I trusted you . . . and you betrayed my trust.'

The condemnation in his voice lashed deeply into Amanda's soul. It stung, yet shock anaesthetised the sting momentarily. Shock demanded explanations that would make sense of the unbelievable.

'You're supposed to be entombed in the crystal caves.' That was the reality that had tortured her. Questions tumbled from her lips. 'How did you get out? How did you escape? How did you get here?'

'How much satisfaction it must have given you to leave me to die as you thought...'

'I did everything I could to try and save you,' she defended hotly, aghast that he had interpreted her actions so wrongly.

'How clever you are, Amanda,' he said sardonically. 'Twisting the truth of your flight down the mountain to give yourself another chance to justify your father's behaviour.'

His offensive manner riled her into pointing out a few little truths to be taken into account. 'You set out to deceive me from our first meeting and you've obviously deceived me about no-one knowing where we were. You were never really in trouble, were you?'

His silence goaded her on. 'And I almost killed myself trying to save you, worrying myself sick over whether you were dead or alive, while all the time... all the time...'

She was rendered speechless by the base calculations of the man who was now revealed as Xa Shiraq himself! There must have been another way out of the caves and he'd had some means of communicating with his people. That was why the helicopter had flown towards the peak... to collect him! He had been flown home in comfort, perhaps even seeing her manic ride on the way.

'Do you think I can still be seduced by your lies?' he demanded. 'You knew I would stop you from doing what you wanted and you sacrificed me for the secret of the crystal caves.'

It focused Amanda's mind on refuting the abominable idea of base treachery. 'I did not! The hydraulic jack broke. I rode for help but you ordered people not to listen to me,' she flung at him, outraged that he could accuse her of such dreadful things—premeditated murder, no less—when he was so palpably at fault for reacting in a totally extreme and unjustified manner, making her suffer agonies for a crime she hadn't committed.

'Nor will I listen to you now,' he bit out in icy, arrogant pride.

'Examine the jack,' she challenged in similar biting tone, glaring her scorn for his unreasonable stance.

'I disdain to prove more clearly what is already proved.'

'How can you call yourself just if you will not look at the evidence?' Amanda retaliated, smarting over the fact that he had always been in control, never once risking anything while he tested her to the limit!

'Be thankful I choose not to.' His eyes seared her with a blistering indictment. 'I prefer mercy to justice. If your perfidy were proved beyond all doubt I could show you no mercy at all.'

Amanda felt a quiver of fear. She suppressed it, and took another pace forward. 'Are you too proud to face the truth?' she hurled at him. 'Is it your will to believe the worst of me? I thought more of you as a man than that.'

His lips compressed into a thin, bloodless line. His facial muscles tightened grimly. 'You cannot hurt me with your words,' he said, his black eyes boring into her with hard and unrelenting intensity. 'I admired and respected your cleverness, the quick facility of your mind at seeing through to the end of what was possible. But you have used it against me.'

He *was* hurt. Deeply hurt. The realisation slammed into Amanda's heart and pumped a different perception through her mind. This was why he was so unyielding. He had let himself be vulnerable to her and he hated her for supposedly fooling him, and himself for being fooled.

'All my thoughts and energies were directed to finding and bringing back a rescue team to get you out,' she said quietly, hoping to reach into him again. 'I couldn't move that huge rock. I had no choice but to leave you there until ...'

'You had a choice, Amanda. I gave it to you in the caves ... whether to reveal the existence of the neodymite crystals as your father wanted ... or whether to leave Xabia the way it is,' he reminded her savagely. 'You did not give a reply.'

'I needed time to think.'

It must have seemed to him ... afterwards ... that she had fobbed off giving a reply, but Amanda knew it wasn't true. When he had kissed her and asked her to give herself to him, that had seemed more important than bringing up something she had already decided and was no longer an issue between them.

'I had made up my mind to keep the secret and let my father's dream die with him,' she pleaded. 'I would have told you so once we were outside.'

Even as she spoke the words she realised it was too late to say them. The wrong time and the wrong place. There would never be a right time now. For years she had worked towards the goal of clearing her father's name and proving him right. That single-minded purpose was burned into Xa Shiraq's memory, reinforced by what she had done and all she had poured out to him in the intimacy of their togetherness.

'I showed you the crystal caves,' he said simply. 'And you betrayed my trust and left me to die in darkness.'

Amanda cracked. She lifted her hands to her face in despair. 'That's so untrue,' she cried brokenly. 'So untrue.'

'You've had a taste of the choice you could have made *with* me. Now you can have a taste of the choice you made *for* me.'

'You've got it all wrong.' It was a desperate bid for understanding. She pulled her hands down, spreading them out to him in appeal. 'Surely what we felt together meant as much to you as it did to me. How can you imagine I would sacrifice that for...?'

She faltered under the terrible look in his eyes ... the pain ... the dull, black emptiness that followed it.

'You will be placed in the deepest cellar of the lowest basement within the granary that supplies the palace,' he intoned, as though he had pulled a hood of judgement over any last twinge of feeling he had for her. 'There are no windows. There is no light. You will be in darkness...as I was in darkness...when you left me.'

Amanda shivered, remembering the claustrophobic feeling in the tunnel. 'I don't like being alone.'

'You will not be alone,' he said with dark derision.

'Who...?' She swallowed hard and tried to correct the quaver in her voice. 'Who will be with me?'

'The cellar has another name. A sobriquet. It is more commonly known as...the rat-hole. The rats are huge. They are voracious. I hope you will enjoy your new friends and acquaintances.'

CHAPTER FIFTEEN

AMANDA stared at Xa Shiraq in glazed horror. Her skin prickled in revulsion. Her stomach turned queasy. Beads of sweat broke out on her forehead. Her hands went clammy. Her whole body shuddered.

'You can't do that to me,' she whispered. It was the only defence her mind could construct against the terrifying picture he had drawn of the rat-hole. She would go insane in such a place.

The black eyes glittered with vengeful satisfaction. 'Call the escort, Kozim,' came the merciless command.

'No...no!' Amanda cried, turning a frantic look of appeal to Xa Shiraq's personal aide. 'I'm innocent of this charge. I swear it!'

Mr Kozim's gaze determinedly evaded hers. He picked up a bell from his desk and rang it loudly. He obviously didn't want to hear any more from her.

Amanda swung back to Xa Shiraq, her heart pounding in sheer panic. 'You're supposed to know everything. That's what they say of you. Why don't you know I couldn't do what you accuse me of?' she argued, hoping against hope he meant to relent.

He pointedly shunned her, walking off to a leather armchair on the far side of the library. He flung himself listlessly and dispiritedly into it without so much as a glance at her. His eyes focused on some empty spot on the ceiling.

Amanda heard the doors opening behind her, the tramp of military feet coming to take her away to the rat-hole. She couldn't bear it.

Xa Shiraq waved a gesture of dismissal towards her.

He should know better, Amanda thought, her mind racing to find some solution. He would never do this if his emotions weren't involved. But they were... they were!

'Wait!' Amanda cried imperiously, raising her extended arm above her shoulders.

It stopped nothing. The military feet kept advancing. Xa Shiraq ignored her. Mr Kozim found another empty spot on the ceiling for himself and gazed steadfastly at that.

Amanda was thinking more furiously than she had ever needed to before. Xa Shiraq might have submerged the link he felt with her but it had been a powerful, compelling link. Somehow she had to find that link again.

'I have a better plan,' she announced.

Boldness be my friend, she prayed wildly. If there was any substance in the form of address used by the old serving woman, she had to have some chance of changing what was happening.

The guards halted around her in escort position, ready to about-turn and take her out as soon as the order was given. Amanda swiftly forestalled the order.

'Will you not allow me one last word?' she demanded of Xa Shiraq.

His black eyes slashed at her. His fingers pressed savagely into the armrest, indenting the cushioned leather one by one, back and forth. He said nothing. The guards remained at attention. Amanda seized on the tacit permission to advance on Mr Kozim.

'Is it constitutionally correct that a princess can be sent to the rat-hole?' she asked, pulling his gaze down from the ceiling.

Mr Kozim not only looked sheepish but very, very unhappy at being chosen to interpret the sheikh's will.

'Over the centuries,' he said ponderously, 'more princesses ended up in the rat-hole, per capita of population, than any other category of our people. It was . . . uh . . . standard procedure in cases of . . .' he coughed ' . . . rebellious intransigence.'

That certainly fitted, Amanda thought, but did the rest follow? 'Am I a princess?' she pressed.

'A proclamation was signed that you were to be treated as such,' Mr Kozim mumbled, shooting a worried glance at the sheikh.

Uh-huh! Amanda thought with satisfaction. A chink in the armour. Xa Shiraq was in two minds about her. Or rather, his heart was warring with his head. He wanted his people to honour her even as he condemned her as unworthy of being his true companion.

His mind was set on punishment to fit the crime he believed she had committed against him, but it wasn't what he really wanted. Not deep down. He wanted the fulfilment of the promise that had shimmered through both of them in the crystal caves. And so did she.

Clutching that conviction to her heart, Amanda walked across the room to where Xa Shiraq indolently lounged, her clear aquamarine eyes reflecting strong and unwavering purpose.

'There has to be a better way of resolving what is between us,' she said.

'Name one,' he invited, his face stonily closed to her, his eyes watchful but giving nothing away.

She knelt beside the armrest of his chair, close enough so that only he could hear her words. 'Tell me of your secret desires and passions,' she said softly, caringly, her eyes openly promising an answer to them.

'I do not desire you,' he replied curtly, contemptuously. 'You could not provoke it in me.'

Amanda refused to be deterred. 'Let me try to change your mind,' she persisted, trying to bore past his wounded pride to the primitive mating instinct that yearned for fulfilment.

His hand curved over the end of the armrest, his long, restless fingers lying still. She lifted her hand and stroked her fingers over the bare skin of his. She saw the sudden tightening of his neck muscles, the leap of his pulse at the base of his throat. He sprang to his feet, whipping his hand out from under hers. He towered over her, his black eyes ablaze with fierce turbulence.

'You do have the capacity to gall me,' he grated. 'No more of this talk. You know nothing of men nor of their pleasure.'

'How can you pass such judgements?' Amanda immediately replied, whirling up off her knees to confront him head-on.

'At the Fisa hotel you inflicted on me a fat cow from the bazaar whose dancing was supposed to entertain me,' he mocked savagely. 'She bored me more thoroughly than I've ever been bored in my life.'

'I can do much better than the fat cow from the bazaar,' Amanda promised quickly, thinking any promise was better than the rat-hole.

His eyes derided her claim. 'Are you suggesting you are not culturally inept?'

'I chose the fat cow from the bazaar for other reasons than entertaining you,' Amanda excused.

'You have the temerity to remind me of your duplicity?'

'I have no trouble remembering yours,' she retorted. 'I also remember the link that crossed those barriers. I doubt that even you can crush that memory.'

His eyes burned into hers, seeking truth, doubting her integrity. 'You want another way to resolve things between us,' he said softly, a dangerous glitter leaping into the black blaze. 'Something other than the justice of the rat-hole.'

'Your justice is blind.'

'Then open my eyes, Amanda . . . by dancing for me.'

He was calling her bluff. If she didn't do better than the dancer she had chosen for him in Fisa, she would end up in the rat-hole. Amanda figured she had one advantage. However bad her dancing might be, he would not be bored if she could stir the desire he was so determinedly repressing.

'How many veils would you allow me?' she asked.

He raised one finger.

It didn't give her much to use in the way of teasing or tantalising. Not that she was particularly adept at that. In fact, she wasn't adept at all in the ancient art of seduction. But she would try.

This was more a mental challenge than a physical one, she assured herself. If she was to prolong her time with him while she danced, what she needed was the longest veil in the world. She also needed time to learn what had to be done.

'Agreed,' she said. Already she was quickly plotting a few more moves she could make to break down his present resistance to her.

His eyes narrowed into slits. He obviously didn't trust her one bit. 'Do not think my admiration for your cleverness will cloud my vision, Amanda. You have much to prove to me. As a woman.'

The rat-hole wouldn't have proved anything, Amanda thought petulantly, but she wisely held her tongue on that matter. She had won a stay in judgement. Better to leave him now while the going was good.

'I'll need time to prepare,' she said.

'Undoubtedly,' he dryly agreed, stepping back and waving her to join her escort again. 'Send a messenger to me when you are ready. Remember I await the outcome of your... plan... with some disbelief.'

'Thank you for the reprieve,' Amanda said with every air of confidence, and gave Mr Kozim a friendly nod as she resumed her place in the middle of her elite squad of soldiers.

The command was given to return her to her quarters.

Amanda found her legs were quite wobbly once they had left the library but she managed to keep them moving, one after the other, until they had traversed the necessary distance.

After all, a princess didn't collapse in a heap when the going got rough. A princess was supposed to be tough. A princess held her head high and sailed through the storm to a safe port.

If she was to be a princess she had to find precisely the right sail to get her there.

Amanda's practical mind descended from the clouds.

It wasn't the right sail she needed.

It was the right veil!

CHAPTER SIXTEEN

KNOWING she had been officially proclaimed a princess gave Amanda the confidence to issue a few orders.

For a start, she was not going to be pushed around by a pack of women who thought they knew more about her body than she did. She took a leaf out of Xa Shiraq's book. They could carry out *her* will instead.

Once she was back in the royal quarters, she ordered a good solid brunch; sausage, fried tomatoes and a piece of buttered toast. After the episode with the sheikh she was not hungry but she forced herself to eat some fruit to stiffen up her wobbly knees. If she was to deliver the performance of her life, energy was a necessary requirement.

The matter of the veil was more complex. Amanda ordered bolts of filmy cloth in shades of blue and green and silver to be brought to her. They were the colours *he* had suggested at Fisa.

Amanda intended to please. She had a vested interest in pleasing him. If she could, she would make him eat his words about her not knowing anything about a man's pleasure.

In a way, Xa Shiraq was right. Amanda had received no advice on such matters from her mother who had died before Amanda had reached the age of puberty.

At the school she had attended during her teenage years, the list of attainments thought desirable for a modern woman did not include any knowledge on how to please a man. The general attitude was that if it did happen, it would occur naturally all by itself.

The natural occurrences that had come Amanda's way in later years had not taught her much. She hadn't been particularly pleased herself, and it seemed that all that was required of her was her consent. Being kissed by Xa Shiraq had been totally different to anything she had experienced before.

Amanda had the feeling that Xa Shiraq would be much more demanding in his pleasure than anyone she had met before, both in giving it and receiving it. If she kept thinking of the feelings he had aroused while kissing her, it might help her to stop worrying about what response she was drawing from him while she did whatever was going to be done.

By the time her tiny appetite was fully satisfied, an extraordinary number of bolts of cloth had been lined up for her to view. With the fear of the rat-hole ever present in the background, and her poor, sick, empty stomach nicely filled, Amanda considered this matter of dancing her way out of trouble and into the heart of Xa Shiraq where she rightfully belonged.

The reflection that she shouldn't be in this trouble at all pricked a little resentment. The manner in which Xa Shiraq had dismissed her sufferings as though they were nothing pricked quite a lot more. To balance that, her crimes of illegal entry into the country, and the charges of grand larceny seemed to have been forgotten. She hoped the unfortunate experiences on the Gemini Peak would also soon be forgotten.

What she could not forget was all the hours he had kept her in a waiting torment of ignorance as to his fate. It seemed absolutely fair to her that he do his share of waiting for her. Besides, being trapped in the caves like that—she shuddered—had obviously tormented his mind about her.

He needed time to consider all she had said in her defence this morning. He needed time to come to the conclusion he must have the hydraulic jack examined, and then more time to adjust to the fact that he was wrong, and she truly loved him.

That might assist him to be more receptive to her, and stop this terrible misunderstanding between them. She wanted to be his lover, not his murderer.

She cast her eyes over the bolts of cloth, then sent for a messenger.

'Please inform Xa Shiraq that there is no cloth in the sheikhdom in shimmering shades of blue and green that meet my requirements. Mindful of his pleasure, I request permission to order that some be dyed to the desired colouring I need. The process will only take several days.'

Then, of course, the veil would have to be made. Amanda's agile mind thought up several more delays, as well. The looms would break. The woof and warp would be wrong. The series of delays she could invent would know no bounds.

She was tempted to add a rider to the message that he should use the time to have the broken hydraulic jack examined, but decided not to raise that sore point yet again. Perhaps, tomorrow. Or the day after.

Amanda was humming happily to herself when the messenger returned with a reply from Xa Shiraq.

"'Permission granted. Be prepared to leave with your escort within the hour. Enjoy your stay in the rat-hole until the dyeing process is completed.''"

Amanda's delightful little bubble of hopes and plans burst into droplets of despair.

But Amanda was a fighter. She would not go down without making a stand. If she was going to be submerged for the third time, she was determined to take someone down with her. That person was Xa Shiraq.

'Please inform Xa Shiraq that a suitable cloth has now been procured. The women who will do the silver thread-work require me for fittings to ensure their design will be pleasing to his discriminating eye. Since there is no light in the rat-hole, I request permission to remain in these quarters until such time as the veil is ready to be worn to its best effect for his pleasure.'

Let him argue against that, Amanda thought with satisfaction. She could spin out the silver embroidery for a good few days. Perhaps a week. Clearly his vengeful mood was still in full force.

The longer she held out, the more likely he might have second thoughts about what had happened.

His reply did not exactly demonstrate that a softening process had begun.

' "Thread or no thread, you will dance for me at midnight tonight." '

Midnight!

Amanda checked the current time. Almost three o'clock. He had given her nine hours. If she didn't deliver what she had promised to his satisfaction at his deadline, Amanda had little doubt she would endure the same fate as many illustrious princesses before her. Xa Shiraq was not a man to be crossed lightly.

Amanda gave her reply much deep thought. Xa Shiraq had to be forcibly reminded of what they had shared together before they met tonight. Amanda's understanding of his grievances only stretched so far. If he didn't open his mind and heart to her again, they would both end up very lonely people.

The prospect of that inner darkness weighed more heavily on Amanda's heart than the prospect of future darkness.

She addressed the messenger one last time.

'Tell Xa Shiraq that the women's fingers grow more nimble by the minute. His will shall be done.

'Then you are to advance upon him. You are to tell him the words you utter cannot be said aloud, and they are for him alone.

'When permission is given, you will whisper to him in tones of love—*May the stars shine brightly for us tonight.*'

CHAPTER SEVENTEEN

KOZIM shifted uncomfortably in his chair as the messenger returned for the third time.

Xa Shiraq was being highly unpredictable today. Many silences had lasted longer than five minutes. Kozim was deeply stressed.

It was clear to him that the geologist's daughter was having a very strange effect on the sheikh. What had seemed an absolutely firm decision about the rat-hole had not turned out a firm decision at all.

How was he to understand anything if everything kept changing? It had been alarming enough when the geologist's daughter had turned to him for succour, although Kozim assured himself he had acted creditably. It was even more alarming to witness Xa Shiraq's reaction to her messages.

The first one had evoked a burst of derisive laughter. Kozim had not thought it a laughing matter. The message had sounded quite impertinent to him. However, the sheikh's reply had certainly put the geologist's daughter in her rightful place. Kozim had heartily approved of that.

To Kozim's mind, the second message should have earned the same result. Xa Shiraq had mused over it, a knowing smile lurking on his lips, his black eyes glittering with calculations. He did not share them with Kozim. His reply, when it came, seemed an extraordinary concession.

Kozim had found it extremely difficult not to expose his surprise. He reflected that the sheikh's mind often worked in mysterious ways. Yet there was a lack of consistency over this business with the geologist's daughter that Kozim found disturbing.

The messenger had barely finished bowing when the sheikh commanded her to speak, not waiting for the usual form of salutations and address.

Xa Shiraq's obvious impatience, indeed, his air of anticipation to hear what the geologist's daughter had to say, was unlike any manner Kozim had witnessed in his long years of service with the sheikh.

The messenger intoned the words.

'Go on. Go on,' Xa Shiraq urged, waving his arms in encouragement. 'There must be more. She would not leave it there.'

The messenger advanced. 'These words are for your ears only.' They were whispered in his ear.

For some reason Kozim could not fathom, Xa Shiraq was so struck by this private communication, his unusual burst of mobility was instantly cut dead. He went absolutely still. Kozim recognised the quality of stillness. It was always thus when the sheikh was absorbing every shade, every minute detail, every nuance of an important problem.

He remained in this state of intense introspection for several minutes, revealing nothing of his thoughts.

'Did the princess say anything else?'

The question ended the long, tense silence.

'No, Your Excellency,' the messenger smartly replied.

'Then you may go.'

The messenger's departure did not end Kozim's growing sense of insecurity. Several more minutes passed before the sheikh deigned to notice him.

'Is there a full moon tonight?' he asked in a voice that rang with decision.

'No, Your Excellency. What moon there is will set before midnight.'

Kozim had already checked his calendar. It was said that a full moon could induce a temporary madness in a man who was under the spell of a woman. Kozim had thought it worth checking if such a dangerous phase was looming on the horizon.

'Order the freshest and finest samples of Xabian jasmine, Kozim. I want it placed in every room.'

'I will see to it,' Kozim said, wondering if partial moons could have the same ill effect.

There was a gleam in the sheikh's black eyes that confirmed Kozim's suspicions. However, if what followed after midnight did not live up to the sheikh's expectations... Kozim thanked his lucky stars he was not the geologist's daughter!

CHAPTER EIGHTEEN

FRUSTRATION edged into desperation as Amanda tried one experiment after another with the veil. She had done a course in pareu tying as practised by the Polynesians. The only difference between a pareu and a veil was that the latter was more diaphanous. She had thought one style or another would produce a desirable effect but none of them did.

What was fine on a tropical beach simply did not have the seductive elegance she was searching for. She needed to entrance, to enthrall. She didn't think she could achieve that by looking...obvious.

The harem women followed her activities with amused interest and much chatter. Amanda felt she was in centre ring of a circus. Irritation added to her edginess and despair. 'Do any of you have a better idea?' she demanded, discarding her last effort as utterly hopeless for her purpose.

The old woman who spoke English rose from a settee. 'Gaia,' she said with a confident air of authority.

The other women clapped with enthusiastic excitement.

Amanda had no idea what it meant. 'I want help,' she said.

The old woman nodded approval and sent off a messenger.

Amanda pulled a robe over her nakedness and sat down to wait for whatever was going to eventuate. She felt totally dispirited. The one-veil idea was a disaster and she was only too aware that her ability to outdance the woman from the Fisa bazaar was pure fantasy. She closed her eyes and imagined the blistering scorn in Xa Shiraq's. She prayed for mercy.

A hubbub from the harem women aroused her attention. A small, sharp-nosed woman was being ushered into the salon of the royal quarters. She was brought to Amanda and introduced by the old woman who had sent for her.

'This is Gaia. She is the best one-veil designer in Alcabab. She has a national and international reputation.'

Gaia's eyes were as sharp as her nose. She made a shrewd appraisal of Amanda as she bowed. Then she stepped back and clapped her hands. It was the signal for an entourage of models to parade in a dazzling variety of single veils, long flowing designs that hid all and revealed everything.

Amanda ruefully realised how amateurish her own efforts must have seemed compared to the sophisticated creations that were being displayed for her benefit. She should have asked for help sooner.

As the last of twenty models filed past, Gaia came forward to inquire, 'Which design would the princess prefer?'

Amanda shook her head, too dazed to make a decisive selection. They were all superb, far beyond anything she could conceive.

'You are right,' Gaia declared, bewildering Amanda with this interpretation of her silence. 'If you are to win the sheikh's heart forever, Princess, only the best will do.'

Like a grand impresario she snapped her fingers and the door to the salon opened once more. A solitary figure entered. All the women gasped in awe and admiration.

'This model,' Gaia said, 'is based upon the exact replica of the one worn by the Queen of Sheba when she arrived at the court of King Solomon.'

It was a brilliant scarlet, looped gracefully over one shoulder where it was fastened by an elaborate gold brooch. From the brooch there fell a rainburst of gold thread, running in cunning diagonals around the model's body, emphasising and high-lighting every feminine curve.

'For you, Princess, it can be copied in shim-mering shades of blues and greens with a silver accent,' Gaia assured her. 'May I respectfully suggest that it is not only appropriate for you to be so dressed, but also essential?'

Palace gossip must have been running hot, Amanda thought. Probably everyone was more aware of what was really going on than she was. But the outfit was absolutely stunning. Amanda felt a stirring of excitement. And hope.

'We use a little artifice,' Gaia explained. 'An in-visible stitch here. An invisible stitch there. Men are so transported by what they see, they never notice.'

'I believe it,' Amanda agreed. A man wouldn't be human if he paused to deliberate on the engineering skills that had put this little number together.

'We have little time, and much to do,' Gaia prompted. 'A design such as this has to be fitted. I have brought my best invisible stitcher with me. The art is to get the best result with the minimum of interference to the natural flowing of the drapery.

'Legend has it that Solomon was so taken by the Queen of Sheba, he granted her all she desired,' Gaia continued. 'Your entrance to the sheikh's quarters must effect the same result so that legend can repeat itself.'

'I hope so,' Amanda said fervently.

'Come with me,' Gaia demanded, leading Amanda into the next room where her assistants waited with the necessary materials for Amanda's requirements. 'My art must remain a secret,' Gaia explained, closing the door on the harem women.

Amanda's robe was quickly removed. She was draped in shimmering blues and greens, the material measured for the length needed for the design. Busy hands fluttered around her, tucking, adjusting, smoothing.

Gaia pointed to a bolt of midnight blue silk taffeta. 'You will require a cloak. This will be most suitable. We shall attach a hood so that your initial presentation will be one of hidden mystery.'

Amanda eagerly agreed to the idea. 'Who pays for all of this?' she asked a little nervously.

'No...o...o problem. I will invoice the palace.'

More crimes, Amanda thought, but she had no choice but to put herself completely into Gaia's hands. She needed all the help she could get.

Under Gaia's private ministrations, Amanda found the time flying all too rapidly. In between fittings of the veil and the cloak she attended to the rest of her appearance. She bathed and had her hair washed and dried and brushed until it shone and felt like silk. The harem women persuaded her to have her body rubbed with a lotion that made her skin glow. Her nails were manicured and varnished an opalescent pink. She eschewed exotic make-up in favour of a subtle highlighting of her eyes and a lip gloss that matched the colour of her nails.

'What of the dance?' Gaia asked. 'Do you need instruction?'

It was clearly in Gaia's interests that Amanda did not let the designer down by failing in other areas.

'I have a plan,' Amanda answered, projecting a confidence she didn't really feel. She knew there simply weren't enough hours to turn her into a skilled dancer, no matter how masterly the instruction. What happened between her and Xa Shiraq would depend on a dance of the mind and heart.

Midnight approached.

The veil was a triumph of erotica by the time Gaia finished arranging it to emphasise and enhance Amanda's curves. Amanda had never thought of herself as a *femme fatale* but she certainly began to see what had induced King Solomon to dally with the Queen of Sheba. There was a definite art to looking and feeling sensual and seductive.

The midnight blue cloak was carefully lowered over her shoulders so as not to disarrange the effect of the veil. Her hair was gathered back and hidden by the hood which formed a shadowy frame for her face. Amanda practised undoing the fastening at her throat so she could open it in one fluid movement.

I'm ready, she told herself. *As ready as I'll ever be.*

She took several deep breaths.

Her nerves were playing havoc with her stomach. Her nipples had tightened into hard little buds. Her thighs were aquiver. She was sure her blood had turned to water.

The clock ticked on.

Near midnight her escort arrived to take her to the sheikh. Her attendants' well wishes rang hollowly in her ears. Gaia accompanied her to the door that led out of the harem. 'My princess ... my queen ...' she whispered, a last benediction that Amanda desperately hoped was prophetic.

With her heart pounding a painful yearning for everything to turn out right, Amanda stepped out of the harem and moved towards her fateful encounter with Xa Shiraq.

CHAPTER NINETEEN

THE doors softly closed behind her. Amanda stood in a circle of light cast by two wall-lamps. The rest of the room receded into darkness. She was spotlit as she had been in their original meeting at the Oasis Hotel in Fisa. It made her feel like a rabbit trapped in the headlights of a car with nowhere to escape.

Where was he?

Music was playing. Soft, romantic music.

In front of her was a magnificent room thickly carpeted in royal blue, with rich furnishings in the same colour combined with white and gold...deeply cushioned sofas in velvet and silk brocade, beautifully grained marble tables, exotic lamps, gold urns holding luxurious plants, exquisite vases from which trailed arrangements of tiny white flowers.

Xabian jasmine.

The scent was unmistakable, stirring Amanda's senses, arousing a tingle of anticipation, soothing her fears. Her pulse quickened. Surely it meant he wanted her to be excited. Or was he teasing her with what could have been?

At the far end of the room was a row of high, graceful arches. Beyond them was total darkness.

'Do you call that a veil?'

The mocking question had a cutting edge to it that sliced into Amanda's assurance in her appearance. So much for an air of mystery!

Her trembling hands went to the fastening at her throat. With the one fluid motion she had practised, the cloak parted. She pushed back the hood then tossed the long coverall from her shoulders. Her hair dropped like a waterfall of spun silk, caressing the bare skin around her collarbones. She held her hands apart as if in supplication.

'Do you want other men to see me like this?' she asked softly.

She heard the voluble intake of his breath.

Her gaze swung to the source of the sound. His tall, lithe body was framed in the last arch on the right-hand side of the room. He was clothed in a pure white robe and headdress, the black and gold coiled *'iqal* circling his head like a crown. He looked every inch the formidable ruler of Xabia.

Amanda took a few steps away from the circlet of light to merge with her own shadows. It suddenly seemed important to meet him on equal terms, person to person, regardless of dress and position.

His black eyes were hidden but Amanda could feel them riveted on her, burning with intensity.

'If the beauty of your mind reflected the beauty of your body I would love you for an eternity.' There was a curl of contempt in his voice as he tried to vanquish the feelings she was arousing in him.

Amanda knew he was affected, deeply affected by her. But he didn't believe in her, she thought despairingly. Not in her words, her love, her need for him.

He gave a derisive laugh. 'Perhaps it was appropriate that you came wrapped in darkness...a phantom of the night. It hides what is best not seen.'

He was trying to negate what he felt, wish it into nonexistence. Amanda knew she had to reach out to him before he set himself irrevocably on a path that would turn him away from her forever.

'I'm as human as you are,' she said quietly. 'You know it. You've felt it. I didn't come here because you ordered me to. I came because I wanted to. I wanted to be with a man who has aroused passions in me that can never be forgotten. I wanted to...'

'Enough!' The tortured command was driven from his throat by forces he could no longer master.

He said nothing more. He stood utterly still.

Amanda bravely held his gaze, willing him to remember she had chosen to go with him and be with him wherever he led, not knowing he meant to reveal the crystal caves to her.

It seemed that the very air between them thickened and thinned with the sheer force of feeling that flowed and swirled in turbulent currents from one to the other. Amanda sensed a mental shift in him, a decision made or a barrier moved aside.

His gaze dropped from hers, gathering a different intensity as it ran slowly over her body, touching every part, heating her blood, sensitising her skin, making her breasts ache with a swollen heaviness, brushing her nipples into taut peaks, circling her stomach with an erotic sensation that arrowed down to the centre of her womanhood, stirring the warm moistness of desire.

He moved. It was as though he drifted along high-tension wires that were strung between them, each step a tug on her heart, a tremor quaking through her body, a wild exhilaration thrilling her mind. His eyes feasted on her, drawing on her innermost being, *wanting her to be all he desired*.

'Dance for me,' he commanded.

Amanda thrust her breasts forward against the flimsy silk chiffon, wanting to feel the imprint of his hands upon them. She swayed her hips in rhythm with the chords of the Eastern music, conscious of the veil sliding and shimmering with every slow, undulating movement. She felt sensual. She was sensual.

'Dance *with* me,' she invited, holding out her arms to him, her voice throbbing with intense emotion and the deeply felt need to be once more taken into his embrace.

'Never!' he said, halting several paces away from her. 'You twist and turn as it suits you. Prove to me you can keep your word. Dance as you said you would.'

Amanda fought against letting this further evidence of his mistrust hurt her. He didn't want it to be this way. She was sure he didn't. 'I thought it would give you more pleasure,' she appealed, swaying to the music in seductive invitation.

He looked at her with hard, scornful pride. 'Do you know nothing of our culture? For centuries, milleniums, women have danced for the pleasure of men.'

Amanda did not have the skill or knowledge to match his Xabian dancers. To try would only invite derision. She needed to reach him, touch him.

She advanced towards him, uninhibitedly provocative in the way she moved as she pleaded her cause. 'That may be true in Xabia. Where I come from, men dance with their women. It has always been so, not only because it is more equal, but because it gives greater pleasure to both.'

'You are in *my* country,' he reminded her.

Amanda opened her hands in a gesture of giving. *'Are we not beyond race and culture?'* she whispered, repeating the very words he had spoken to her in the Presidential Suite in Fisa, the words that had tapped so powerfully at her resistance to him.

He stiffened. His chin lifted fractionally, tightening as though she had hit him. She sensed the conflict raging within him, the strong impulse to accept what she was offering, against his rigid sense of what was owed to him.

'You said you would dance for me,' he bit out, still holding her to her word.

'For you...with you...so you can feel the dance that is only for you.'

'I would not be able to see you,' he said, dismissing her argument, turning aside in disdainful rejection of it.

She quickly reached out and touched his shoulder, arresting his movement away from her.

He did not pull away but he did not turn back to her, either.

'You will see all you need to see,' she promised huskily. 'You will see my eyes.'

Amanda trailed her hand down his arm. She sensed his struggle to exert control over the desire she stirred in him. Slowly he turned, the swing of his body dislodging her hand so that it dropped away from him. It didn't matter because his eyes told her she had touched him in far more than a physical sense. The violence of his feelings was reflected in their dark turbulence. His chest rose and fell several times before he spoke.

'Your eyes have the depths of oceans, and hold the mystery of the skies. They hold the promise of unknown delights; they would tempt any man...beyond endurance.'

She moved closer to him. 'Take what I can give and give to you alone. Feel my body pulsing in harmony with yours.'

His fingertips bridged the distance between them, barely brushing her waist, yet his touch was magnified by the fineness of the material that barely separated his flesh from hers. An electrifying tingle raced over Amanda's skin. It was as though the shimmering veil transmitted the compelling power of his desire for her, making her body more responsive, more aware than if she'd been naked.

Amanda knew she had to show this man she loved him. He had to know it beyond all doubt. Only by giving him the absolute assurance that she held nothing back from him, now or ever, would he come to a true appreciation of what she felt for him.

She let the music seep into her body, breathed deeply of the intoxicating jasmine scent and moved forward, undulating against him, provoking, prompting, her thighs sliding over his, the tips of her breasts rolling across his chest, and not for one second did her eyes leave his, challenging him to see, to know, to believe.

His loins hardened into rigidity.

The fingertips at her waist drifted down, tracing the curve of her hip, then slowly tempted to move over the soft mound of her buttocks. His other hand joined the voyage of discovery, caressing her back, following the sensual curve of her spine. She shivered in his arms and saw the leap of exultant pleasure in his eyes, the knowledge that her response was beyond any design or control.

Amanda slid her own hands over his shoulders, under the flowing headdress, finding and stroking the bare nape of his neck. A muffled cry was torn from his lips. He gripped her body more firmly, moving it to the rhythm she had incited in his, crushing her breasts against the hard masculinity of his chest.

Amanda felt the heat suffusing her body, becoming concentrated between her thighs, the sharpening awareness and piercing sensitivity growing, strengthening, spiralling towards involuntary orgasm, and her eyes clung to his, mirroring the sweet drowning inside her, her lips parting on a gasp of wonder, a breath of life that she offered to him as a gift of utter abandonment to the feelings he evoked in her.

If he could see her heart, he must know it pounded for him.

If he could see her mind, he must know he obliterated everything else.

If he could see her soul, he must know he resided there.

'Amanda...'

It was a whisper of seeing and knowing and believing. He carried it to her parted lips, his mouth closing over hers, warm, sensual, the breath of his life mingling with hers, so softly, caringly, nurturing her gift of love with infinite tenderness, tasting it as though it was the most exquisite wine in the world, incredibly, wonderfully, uniquely intoxicating.

His fingers found the brooch that fastened the veil. With a single movement he unclipped it. He parted the flowing panels, baring her shoulder, and his mouth moved from hers, trailing soft burning kisses down her throat. Instinctively, Amanda arched her neck to the beat of his pleasure. Her hands moved restlessly, throwing off his headdress in her need to touch more of him, her fingers revelling in the silky thickness of his hair.

He eased the chiffon over her breasts with his tongue, absorbing the texture of her skin, sensitising it to his taste, leaving her with hot, licking imprints of himself that burned into a deeper possession of her consciousness. As the veil undraped and slid from her hips he followed it, adoring her body, the revelation of her nakedness, her satin-smooth flesh, all the way down until what the Queen of Sheba had once worn lay as a pool of formless cloth about her feet.

Agile fingers, never still in their ceaseless roaming, sent ripples of pleasure down her thighs. His mouth began its relentless march up her body towards the object of his pleasure. Amanda felt herself going limp, overwhelmed by the almost unendurable sensations he was evoking. She had to restrain herself from crying out in case it made him cease his exquisite ministrations.

Her breasts heaved. Her legs trembled. In a flowing motion he picked her up into the warmth of his arms, cradling her across the strong wall of his chest. Amanda was beyond caring where he took her. She clung to him, wanting him with a deep, desperate ache that yearned to be filled by this man and only this man.

He carried her through the archway to a terrace, and here the scent of the Xabian jasmine was stronger. The air was warmer, more sensual. Amanda could see the sky. The stars were brightly shining.

He lowered her on to an opulently cushioned dais, thickly strewn with the soft petals of wild mountain roses. Fronds of freshly cut jasmine leaves formed a semicircle around her upper body. The realisation that this had all been prepared for her was sweet confirmation of her faith in the feelings they had shared together. He had hoped...dreamed...wanted...and like a gently wafting summer breeze his fingers caressed her waiting breasts.

'Come to me,' she moaned. 'Love me!'

His clothes were tossed aside. Her eyes feasted on his physical beauty. He was perfectly proportioned, his body sleekly honed to tight flesh stretched over the curves of muscles that were strongly delineated. The smooth sheen of his skin looked like polished bronze in the starlight. She was enthralled by the power of his maleness, the visible pulsing of his need for her.

She was aflame with desire. She did not try to hide her willing receptivity and need for his embrace. She lay fully exposed, her back arched in anticipation, her arms outflung across the cushions in complete abandon.

He came to her like a man who had ceased to function for anything other than joining with her. He slid between her legs. With a hoarse cry he plunged deeply into her body. Amanda felt a fierce and triumphant satisfaction as at last their union was completed. She closed around him, squeezing, a wild, exultant joy pleasuring along his manhood.

A gasp of astonishment emitted from his lips. Amanda felt a sense of exaltation. She knew he had not experienced anything like this before in his life. She was putting her imprint on him, possessing him as no other woman had or would, making him as deeply hers as she was his . . . linked forever by this moment of mating.

He started a fierce stroking that super-heated her inflamed responses. Her thighs trembled. Her body tap-danced to the beat of his rhythm and her need for climactic release. She gasped involuntarily as a suffusion of moisture melted around his pulsing flesh.

Xa Shiraq appeared to take it as some kind of signal. His back was arched like a bow, his weight supported by his extended arms, as he drove faster and deeper and faster within her. His breathing came in short gasps, feral and unrestrained. Amanda convulsed around him again. Short, rapid, staccato thrusts preceded a guttural exclamation of appeasement and release as the innermost seeds of his passion spilled from his body into hers.

Instinctively Amanda's arms reached up to hug him and bring him closer to her. She had to be close to him now, closer than she had ever been. She had to prove her love and want and need for him. He had to know that he was the one.

He did not resist. His torso met hers and he cradled her in his arms. His lips brushed across her forehead, her temples, her cheeks, her mouth.

He rolled to one side, carrying her with him, then onto his back so that she lay on top of him. He rested her head upon his shoulder, their bodies still connected although the first rush of desire had been appeased.

'Be at peace with me,' he murmured.

His hands moved over her back and shoulders while applying a sweetly scented lotion to her tingling skin. His strokes were long and languorous and mesmerising, weaving another dimension of intimacy. Amanda felt herself relax under the spell of his hypnotic touch. He drew gentle, entrancing patterns over her body, down her arms, even to her fingers so that every part of her that was accessible to him was caressed into tranquillity.

Amanda was almost asleep from his gentle pleasure-giving when she felt him stir and quicken inside her. She did nothing. Curiosity as to what he would do and how he would behave towards her encouraged her to give no visible sign that she was aware of what was happening.

She felt him engorge to his full extent within her. She forced herself to remain limp and relaxed in his arms. She controlled her breathing so that no alteration could be detected.

He found the contours of her breasts and traced their soft fullness with the delicate touch of moon-beams upon a mountain mist.

He stirred within her, yet with the waft of a sigh, his hands moved away from her breasts and onto the cushions beside him. He moved no more, leaving her to her repose.

Amanda waited. His desire for her did not abate. But he did nothing that would awaken her. Slowly she shifted, as though aroused from sleep. She lifted her head close to his ear.

'I had a beautiful dream,' she whispered, 'in which you gave me great pleasure. More pleasure than I ever thought it possible for a woman to have. Now it is my turn to please you.'

She started moving on him until he could bear it no longer. When he had to take control, Amanda did nothing to restrain him. She gave of herself with all the ecstatic bliss of knowing the giving in his heart.

Afterwards, as the stars faded from the skies, they slept together in each other's arms.

CHAPTER TWENTY

KOZIM could barely conceal his bewilderment. Life is change, he told himself, but the changes were so sweeping it was difficult to adjust to them and the rate at which events were unfurling was truly staggering.

The wedding preparations were no problem. Kozim was used to organising huge ceremonial occasions. This, of course, would be the grandest of them all, but there was no set of ordered arrangements he could not handle with ease.

The proclamation that no future queen could be sent to the rat-hole was another matter entirely. It was a complete break from tradition. Not only that, it was to be imbedded in the constitution of the country, turning the proclamation into unbreakable law. Such tampering with history had no precedent. Kozim found it deeply disturbing.

The geologist's daughter, he reflected, had a way of getting things done that he himself had never possessed. Kozim pulled himself up on that thought. It was the princess, not the geologist's daughter. A slip of the tongue on such a point over the future queen could result in the most fateful consequences for himself. He needed to take care. Xa Shiraq was obviously besotted over his wife-to-be.

She certainly had the most voluptuous and exciting body... and the radiance of her hair was entrancing...

Kozim sternly suppressed such thoughts. They could lead to the permanent separation of the head from the body, a punishment he had once favoured, but upon more mature reflection, it seemed as extreme as the rat-hole. Perhaps the mellowing effect that this woman was having on Xa Shiraq was also having an effect upon himself.

Today had been very busy with the sheikh holding open court for his people. The *majlis* had extended into the afternoon and still there was one more deputation to deal with, yet Xa Shiraq appeared amazingly relaxed. His fingers were not tapping like a measured metronome. They seemed to be dancing on the armrest of his chair, in time to some light, frivolous melody.

Kozim shook his head. There was so much that was beyond his comprehension. How Xa Shiraq had changed his mind about the geologi—the princess—and obviously believed her, long before the hydraulic jack was examined, was a total mystery to Kozim. But it had proved right. The device had snapped under the load of that huge rock and the woman was not to blame at all.

Still, Xa Shiraq could very easily have lost his life. If he had not been able to leap the chasm and work his way up through the mountain to the eagle's eyrie, from where he could use the transmitter in his signet ring to summon the helicopter, Xabia could now be without a ruler. Kozim could be without a job. He shuddered at such a terrible prospect.

And all for the sake of gathering those strange crystals for his wife-to-be! It made no sense to Kozim. The crystals were quite pleasant to look at, and for some reason the air about them seemed sweeter and fresher, but obviously they were intrinsically worthless. Why Xa Shiraq had ordered them to be set in gold seemed ... Kozim clamped down on the critical thought. The gold did increase their value. He still thought it a poor wedding gift for the future queen, but undoubtedly the sheikh had his reasons.

Kozim noticed, with alarm, that more than five minutes had passed and Xa Shiraq had not said a word. Kozim gave a nervous little cough. 'I did send a messenger to the princess, Your Excellency,' he said, anxious not to be found at fault.

Xa Shiraq bestowed a benevolent smile. 'It is of no consequence, Kozim. The princess will arrive when she is ready.'

That was another thing that disturbed Kozim. The rigid time-keeping to a planned schedule had suffered considerably since the night of the Queen of Sheba veil. It was totally incomprehensible to Kozim that Xa Shiraq apparently accepted that the princess exercised a will of her own. Kozim did not like to think where such a thing might lead. He consoled himself with the assurance that Xa Shiraq knew everything and it must therefore be a wise course.

The doors to the hall of government opened. Kozim and Xa Shiraq instantly sprang to their feet as the princess entered. She was a vision of rare beauty. She wore a misty lilac gown that flowed enticingly around her very feminine body as she walked forward.

Kozim struggled to pull his thoughts into appropriate order. Of course the gown was supremely modest, whispering down to her feet, and with long graceful sleeves that caressed her soft, shapely arms. The princess was certainly a credit to the sheikh. Kozim had thought the proposed marriage a mistake at first. It would not cement any alliances or extend profitable areas of trade but...no man could possibly look upon the princess for long and continue to think of her as a mistake.

Amanda flashed Mr Kozim a smile as she walked up to meet Xa Shiraq. The stout little man was such a sweet person once one got to know him, a trifle uncertain of himself at times, but she would help him find his feet. He was always so anxious to please, to get everything right. He also thought Xa Shiraq was the fount of all wisdom, which made him invaluable as a personal aide.

She extended a much brighter smile to the man she loved. His eyes were soft black velvet as he greeted her. A smile hovered on his lips, giving them a sensual curve. He took her hand to lead her to the chair that had been set beside his, and Amanda once again marvelled at the pleasure of his touch, the tingling warmth of his skin against hers, the strength and the tenderness of his long, supple fingers.

'Why did you want me here?' Amanda asked, surprised that he should ask her to join him at a *majlis* where he listened to the problems brought to him by his people.

His eyes twinkled wickedly. 'I want you everywhere.'

She laughed. 'Not in front of Mr Kozim. He would definitely be shocked.'

'You are right. I am not sure Kozim can sustain many more shocks. We shall consider his feelings. There is a matter that concerns you.'

He saw her seated, and raised a hand to Mr Kozim as he settled in the chair beside her.

Mr Kozim rang a bell.

The doors opened.

Amanda was mystified as to what the matter could be. Then Mocca came bouncing in, his boyish face beaming with what looked suspiciously like mischievous delight. He performed an elaborate bow, then followed it with a long flattering address, extolling the wisdom *and generosity* of Xa Shiraq.

'You may address the princess,' he was dryly told.

Mocca was not slow to pick up his cue. 'I have come with good news and bad news.'

'What is the bad news?' Amanda asked, wondering if there was another mountainous pile of invoices about to be sent to the palace.

'We could not find the caves for which we were searching,' Mocca announced dolefully.

'Then it is proven that they do not exist,' Amanda declared. 'You have done well, Mocca. I thought it was a wild-goose chase but I wanted to know. Thank you. I am glad the matter is finally settled.'

Xa Shiraq squeezed her hand. She squeezed back. The secret would remain with them.

Mocca's face lit with pleasure. 'In that case,' he said cheerfully, 'there is only good news.'

'What is the good news?' Amanda inquired.

'Your bodyguard has performed an invaluable service for you.'

That was certainly news to Amanda, but she was not confident that it would be good.

'They have caught the man who has been saying the most ridiculous and offensive things about people who have the colour of hair that you have, oh, Princess,' Mocca continued.

Here, too? Amanda thought in exasperation.

'He has been saying you are stupid, you are dumb and you are a female dog.'

Amanda bristled.

Xa Shiraq leaned over and whispered, 'I rejected Charles Arnold's petition to appeal against his dismissal from the Oasis Hotel chain. Apparently he thought that gave him a license to be as offensive as he pleased.'

So that was why Charles Arnold had come to Alcabab. No doubt he was taking out his peevishness by insulting Xa Shiraq's choice of wife. Amanda felt a warm glow of approval for her bodyguard.

'What has my bodyguard done with him?' she asked Mocca.

'As you are aware, people of your hair colouring are much admired in Xabia,' he declared fervently.

'I knew this was a wonderful country,' Amanda declared with equal fervour.

'So we hung a sign of what he'd said around his neck and marched him through the streets. The populace showed their disapproval. They booed him. They pelted him with camel dung...and other evil-smelling refuse.'

'Oh, dear!' Amanda wasn't at all sure he deserved that much humiliation. 'He is a creep and a slime, but I'd better go and see the poor man in case he's damaged.'

'I wouldn't do that if I were you,' Xa Shiraq remarked very dryly.

Mocca flashed him his friendliest grin. 'We also carried out the unspeakable. It felt really good doing it to him.'

A vision of the rat-hole flew into Amanda's mind. She sprang to her feet. 'Take me to him at once!' she commanded.

'Princess!' Mr Kozim started up in alarm.

Xa Shiraq gave Kozim a knowing look as he rose to accompany Amanda. 'There's no stopping her once she gets the bit between her teeth, Kozim. The only thing to do is to satisfy her.'

'Wise. Very wise,' Mr Kozim mumbled, but could not hide his distress at this highly inappropriate turn of events.

Mocca led off through the corridors of the palace. As they approached a courtyard that opened out to one of the gardens, Amanda's nose was assaulted by a revolting smell. She refrained from comment but she privately decided the sewerage system urgently needed updating.

Mocca threw open the door to a room that overlooked the courtyard and stood back for Amanda to see the occupant. The stench was dreadful.

'We painted him with asafoetida,' Mocca proudly announced. 'He can't stand the smell of himself and no-one else can, either. It is the vilest-smelling naturally occurring substance on the planet. Wasn't that a great punishment?'

Charles Arnold was a pitiable sight. He fell to his knees in a grovelling plea for mercy. 'Mandy, for God's sake! Please do something! Help me!'

She fought for breath. 'Mocca...' she gasped, unable to share his boyish delight in the retribution taken, even though it certainly was a powerful deterrent to any human intercourse at all. Charles Arnold did deserve to know what it was like to have nastiness heaped upon him. Nevertheless, enough was enough! 'Take him away... and let him wash it off,' she choked out.

'Oh, thank you, Mandy. Thank you, thank you, thank you,' Charles Arnold raved, clearly at the end of his tether.

Amanda was sharply reminded of the abuse she had suffered from him. 'In future, Charles, please remember that my name is Amanda, not Mandy.'

'Princess Amanda,' Mocca corrected, 'and very soon to be Her Majesty,' he added for good measure. Then he clapped his hands and the bodyguards started streaming in from the courtyard. 'Okay, boys,' he said cheerfully. 'Take him away and throw him into the well from which no-one ever returns.'

'No, no, no!' Amanda cried. 'I meant take him away and give him a scrubbing brush and strong soaps and deodorants . . .' She gasped for breath again. The smell was suffocating. 'I'm sorry, Charles. You are the most offensive person it's ever been my displeasure to meet. Please learn from this experience and treat people decently in the future. I must go now.'

Xa Shiraq took her arm and gave a stern, finishing touch to her command. 'When he is deodorised, Mocca, he is to leave Xabia and never return.'

'Perhaps he need not wash until we see him over the border, Your Excellency,' Mocca suggested eagerly.

Xa Shiraq curbed his enthusiasm. 'Do as your princess commands, Mocca.'

'Yes, yes! Her will is my will. Your will is my will, oh, most gracious and generous . . .'

'How much did you pay him?' Amanda muttered as Xa Shiraq swept her away from the putrid area.

He chuckled. 'Such an enterprising young man deserves a reward. He turned a problem into a triumph for you, my love. The populace of Alcabab have taken you into their hearts. There is no greater joy than pelting camel dung at someone who richly deserves it. Perhaps Mocca has even given birth to a future legend. The filthy-tongued foreigner who denigrated the beauty of the Queen...'

Much later that evening Amanda was with Xa Shiraq in his private apartment. She was comfortably curled up on one of the blue velvet sofas as she questioned him about the guests who would be attending their wedding.

'Did you realise that Jebel Haffa is not on the list?' she asked, puzzled by the omission.

Xa Shiraq gave her a bemused little smile. 'I as good as told you, that night in the tent outside the village of Tirham, that Jebel Haffa does not exist.'

Amanda shook her head in astonishment. 'The second most important man in Xabia does not exist?' she repeated incredulously.

'It goes a long way back to the time of troubles. I needed someone who was absolutely loyal to me, whom I could always trust. There was no such person I could find. I invented Jebel Haffa.'

'You said he was part of you,' Amanda mused, more to herself than to him. She realised now how truly he had expressed himself.

'It is why I have had to live a rather reclusive life,' he explained. 'So I could play both roles as necessary. It made a legend live. It made Xabians feel doubly secure.'

The man who was never seen, Amanda thought, except in a black cloak and hood that kept his face in shadow. 'And no-one knows of this?' she asked.

'Not even Kozim.'

'So how will you explain his absence from the wedding?'

'It will be Jebel Haffa's duty to look after the realm during the period of our marriage and honeymoon. When we return, Jebel Haffa will have to die. He has served his function, the role he had to play.'

'I don't want Jebel Haffa to die,' Amanda said. 'He was a wonderful person. He was part of you. Can't he be retired to his country estates?'

Xa Shiraq gave her a rueful smile. 'Enough,' he said. 'You shall have your way. When we return, we will mutually decide Jebel Haffa's fate.'

Xa Shiraq walked over to her, took her hands in his and gently urged her up from the sofa. His arms slid around her, drawing her close. His black eyes shone with a brilliance Amanda had never seen before.

'You are now my Jebel Haffa,' he said softly. 'Only more so, Amanda. Much more so. In you I have found the true companion and partner of my life. In you I place my absolute trust and know you will give me absolute loyalty. As I will give to you. For we are as one, as I was one with him. In mind, in heart, in soul.'

He was completely open to her. No shutters. No veils of mystery. The brilliance of his eyes were the stars of a universe she had yet to explore fully, but it was hers to travel with him, to share, to know and to love.

She curled her arms around his neck and drew his head down to hers. They kissed... tasting the future that was theirs... and the goblet was full.

Coming Next Month

HARLEQUIN PRESENTS®

#1773 LOVE'S PRISONER Elizabeth Oldfield
Piers Armstrong was a newly released hostage—and Suzy wanted to feature him in her new book. But, after all that had happened between them three years ago, would Piers want to do Suzy any favors?

#1774 YESTERDAY'S ECHOES Penny Jordan
Rosie had been seduced at a party when she was a teenager—and Jake Lucas seemed to know all her secrets. Would he despise her for them and shatter the fragile peace she'd fought hard to create in her life?

#1775 NEVER A BRIDE Diana Hamilton (Wedlocked!)
Clare and Jake's marriage was a paper one, based on convenience. Only now Clare had foolishly fallen in love with her husband!

#1776 SLAVE TO LOVE Michelle Reid
Roberta finally realized she'd never be more than Soloman Maclaine's mistress. She had to leave—could she give up their sweet nights of passion?

#1777 HOT NOVEMBER Ann Charlton (Dangerous Liaisons)
Matt MacKenzie had warned Emma that it only took one spark to start a blaze—and there were bushfires everywhere! November was going to be a very hot month indeed...in every sense!

#1778 SCANDALS & SECRETS Miranda Lee
(Book 5 of Hearts of Fire)
The fifth in a compelling six-part saga—discover the passion, scandal, sin and hope that exist between two fabulously rich families.

Celeste Campbell had lived on her hatred of Byron Whitmore for twenty years—and revenge was sweet. But suddenly Celeste found she could no longer deny her long-buried feelings of desire for Byron.... Meanwhile, Gemma realized exactly how much she cared for Nathan—when she heard him talking to his ex-wife, Lenore, as if they were lovers!

MILLION DOLLAR SWEEPSTAKES (III)

No purchase necessary. To enter, follow the directions published. Method of entry may vary. For eligibility, entries must be received no later than March 31, 1996. No liability is assumed for printing errors, lost, late or misdirected entries. Odds of winning are determined by the number of eligible entries distributed and received. Prizewinners will be determined no later than June 30, 1996.

Sweepstakes open to residents of the U.S. (except Puerto Rico), Canada, Europe and Taiwan who are 18 years of age or older. All applicable laws and regulations apply. Sweepstakes offer void wherever prohibited by law. Values of all prizes are in U.S. currency. This sweepstakes is presented by Torstar Corp., its subsidiaries and affiliates, in conjunction with book, merchandise and/or product offerings. For a copy of the Official Rules send a self-addressed, stamped envelope (WA residents need not affix return postage) to: MILLION DOLLAR SWEEPSTAKES (III) Rules, P.O. Box 4573, Blair, NE 68009, USA.

EXTRA BONUS PRIZE DRAWING

No purchase necessary. The Extra Bonus Prize will be awarded in a random drawing to be conducted no later than 5/30/96 from among all entries received. To qualify, entries must be received by 3/31/96 and comply with published directions. Drawing open to residents of the U.S. (except Puerto Rico), Canada, Europe and Taiwan who are 18 years of age or older. All applicable laws and regulations apply; offer void wherever prohibited by law. Odds of winning are dependent upon number of eligibile entries received. Prize is valued in U.S. currency. The offer is presented by Torstar Corp., its subsidiaries and affiliates in conjunction with book, merchandise and/or product offering. For a copy of the Official Rules governing this sweepstakes, send a self-addressed, stamped envelope (WA residents need not affix return postage) to: Extra Bonus Prize Drawing Rules, P.O. Box 4590, Blair, NE 68009, USA.

SWP-H1095

Become a
Privileged Woman,
You'll be entitled to all these Free Benefits. And Free Gifts, too.

To thank you for buying our books, we've designed an exclusive FREE program called *PAGES & PRIVILEGES*™. You can enroll with just one Proof of Purchase, and get the kind of luxuries that, until now, you could only read about.

BIG HOTEL DISCOUNTS

A privileged woman stays in the finest hotels. And so can you—at up to 60% off! Imagine standing in a hotel check-in line and watching as the guest in front of you pays $150 for the same room that's only costing you $60. Your *Pages & Privileges* discounts are good at Sheraton, Marriott, Best Western, Hyatt and thousands of other fine hotels all over the U.S., Canada and Europe.

FREE DISCOUNT TRAVEL SERVICE

A privileged woman is always jetting to romantic places. When you fly, just make one phone call for the lowest published airfare at time of booking— or double the difference back!

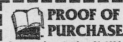

PLUS—you'll get a $25 voucher to use the first time you book a flight AND 5% cash back on every ticket you buy thereafter through the travel service!